The Price of Freedom

Parapraxis
Press TM

Andy is right about one thing: if Scotland were to go its own way, Scottish soldiers would have a decision to make. I'm not sure how it would all go down like, but there are boys out there who are a wee bit serious about it all.
—"T", Argyll & Sutherland Highlanders (now RRS)

Andy portrays many aspects of the Special Regiments very accurately. And there are certainly a lot of Scots in the Regiments as well.
—"P", Special Boat Service

The Price of Freedom

A novel by

Andy Skeen

Parapraxis
Press ™

Andy Skeen

ISBN: 978-0-9567616-2-0

Published by Parapraxis Press™

To the professional Special and Regular Soldiers, Seamen and Airmen of Great Britain, the United States and all their allies who put themselves in harm's way every day.

From the cliffs of Point duc Hoc to the Green Zones and mountains of Afghanistan, and from the jungles of South East Asia to the deserts of the Middle East and North Africa, we owe our liberty, freedoms, security, prosperity, happiness and lives to all of you. Thank you.

And to Wendy for believing ...

Andy Skeen

Contents

Andy Skeen

Acknowledgements

This is a work of fiction, and as such, any and all mistakes are entirely my own. With that caveat in mind I would like to acknowledge the help and input of everyone who read and commented on various drafts. This includes Chris N., Peter R., Andrew B., Sanjog S., Walter S., Alice S., Clive B. and Ben & Sarah B. I couldn't have done this without you!

I would also like to thank my buddies in the SF communities of the UK, US and the RSA. Sorry if I got anything wrong in here chaps! Special thanks to 'Rambo', Sgt. Horn and Drew, you guys are the greatest. Good luck with your book Sgt. Horn!

Andy Skeen

Author's preface

This is just a story and nothing more. It has no other purpose or hidden agenda and I am not actively for or against Scottish independence. My only feeling on the matter is that come what may, the will of the Scottish people should prevail.

The idea for this story began, as so many good ideas do, over pints of Belhaven Best in The Cambridge Bar in Edinburgh. I got to chatting with some Scottish soldiers about what might happen if Scotland ever tried to leave the UK.

Hearing Scottish soldiers in the British Army, of which there are a great many, say very solemnly, that they would "have some decisions to make," set my storytelling mind to spinning. How far would they go? It amazed me how similar the rhetoric of both sides mirrored that which led to the Irish crisis of the early Twentieth Century … and we all know how that ended up.

The political parties in England (at time of writing) sounded certain to challenge the validity of any referendum. I was also intrigued by the revelations about British government actions during the 1970s to thwart Scottish independence and stop them controlling North Sea Oil. I wondered just how far Britain would go to hang onto it. And then, the media started reporting that North Sea Oil wasn't running out nearly as fast as previously thought …

Andy Skeen
Edinburgh, 2012

Andy Skeen

A note on Scots language

In order to keep a flavour of authenticity, the text includes a light smattering of 'Scots' where it seemed appropriate. Scots is used anytime that, in the author's opinion, the character would use a Scots word.

For those unfamiliar with Scots and the Scottish vernacular, here are some of the more common uses:

Nae – no, not
Dinnae – did not, do not
Cannae – cannot
Tae – to
Aye – yes, as in 'Och Aye', oh yes
Ken – know, as in 'dinnae ken', don't know, or 'I ken it', I know it.

Likewise, the characters use profanity as and when a real person would do so. This includes prodigious use of the 'c' word, as both an insult and a term of endearment. This is common among many Scot males, especially soldiers.

Andy Skeen

". . . for so long as a hundred of us remain alive, never will we on any conditions be subjected to the lordship of the English. It is in truth not for glory, nor riches, nor honours that we are fighting, but for freedom alone, which no honest man gives up but with life itself."

Declaration of Arbroath, April 6th, 1320

Andy Skeen

Belfast on the Forth

Edinburgh, Scotland, near future

The sniper pulled back the bolt of the Accuracy International L115A sniper rifle, then eased it forward and down again chambering the heavy .338 Lapua Magnum round. The huge cartridge, something like five times the size of the standard infantry ammunition, would blow a man's head to small pieces. It would easily disable most vehicles, even tanks if it hit the right spot.

His breathing and heart rate remained stable and controlled, he didn't sweat and no random thought disturbed his concentration as he waited for his prey. The fibreglass stock settled comfortably against his shoulder and fit his reach perfectly—just like it had been made for him, which, of course, it had.

The big multi-focal high power scope combined with the special magnum ammunition gave him an effective range of 1.5 kilometres. He knew without thinking that he had twelve .338 Lapua magnum cartridges. He had 'stagger loaded' the magazine with every other cartridge topped with a tungsten armour piercing round, paired with a mushrooming semi-jacketed hollow-point boat-tail round. If his targets didn't leave their hardened, bulletproof vehicles, he wanted the option of the AP round.

To his right, on the west end of Princes Street, a column of Warrior armoured personnel carriers and Scimitar light armoured tanks rumbled into view. They had come from the west having rolled off the heavy transports that had deposited them on the runway at Edinburgh Airport. He knew where they were headed, everyone knew: the Old Parliament building on the Royal Mile where the Scottish Parliament sat in defiance of Westminster's dissolution order. All along Princes Street protestors waved Saltire and Lion Rampant flags, chanted slogans and screamed in anger at the soldiers in the column.

The Prime Minister in Westminster had made a speech calling for calm and warning against terrorism. The sniper didn't consider himself a terrorist though, and what he was about to do wasn't a terrorist act. This was an occupation of a sovereign country and it was his right, nae his *duty,* to defend his homeland. He would hold to Geneva Convention rules and he wouldn't target any non-combatants.

He had his own code as well. He would try to avoid harming any enlisted men who were only following orders. He would target and disrupt the chain of command. English officers would be his prey—senior officers gave the orders and they were responsible. Without them this unlawful invasion would end.

As the Warriors and Scimitars clanked and rumbled along, turning up the Mound, the sniper spotted an armoured staff car festooned with antennae. Inside, he knew, sat the commanding officer of this operation, one General Edward Trentworth. The sniper slowed his breath and started counting his heartbeats focusing his scope on the stern well-bred visage of his target as the man exited his car, batting away a microphone and yelling at a reporter as he did so.

The sniper couldn't risk the shot as he was too near the crowd of civilians, he moved his scope, picking up a staffer trailing behind the General.

He timed his trigger pull between heartbeats, holding his breath so that nothing could take the shot off target. Watching the flags of one of the protesters, he corrected his aim for wind direction and then gently massaged the hair-trigger of his powerful rifle.

It bucked hard in his grip, but he rode the recoil keeping the target within the scope field. He ejected the spent casing and chambered a new round in a swift fluid motion.

An Infantry Captain to the General's right, another squeeze, another recoil. Quick flick of the bolt to load another round. The sniper kept the scope moving, picking up his third target—a Lieutenant huddled giving orders to his platoon sergeants. Another gentle caress of the trigger, another violent recoil. The officer's limp body slumped to the ground, a six-inch hole blown out his back at chest height.

Each bullet cracked as it left the barrel. He knew that was the sound of the round breaking the sound barrier and that the sound barrier was his best friend. Three shots fired and the sound of the rifle had not yet reached the Mound.

The sniper swept the area with his scope, catching sight of a Major, probably the General's number two. The man stood in a daze, gaping around at his falling comrades, not yet registering what was happening. He settled. Another breath exhaled... timed his heartbeat ... and massaged the trigger one last time. The Major's head exploded, spattering bits of bone, blood and brains all over the prostrate and dead soldiers scattered across the ground. Soldiers, now leaderless, cowered on the ground, waiting for the next shot, paralysed with fear.

Ten seconds, four shots. Time to go...

The column of armoured personnel carriers and hardened staff cars made its way along Princes Street. As his car turned up the Mound he could see that the first part of the operation had gone smoothly so far, with many of his men deployed by helicopters on drop ropes, already taking their positions. From his radio he heard confirmation that they were also taking up their positions on the Royal Mile sealing off that entrance.

The demonstrators were angry, but no one seemed to be carrying any weapons. Half the damned city stood in the street and the gardens though. General Edward Trentworth clenched his teeth. He just hoped no one would get hurt in this little exercise, not his men and not any of the politicians who were betraying Britain and their King with their foolishness. He hoped this would come off without any trouble at all.

Half the bloody army had gone AWOL, including nearly all the Scots of course, including nearly the entire Royal Scots, one of the largest front-line infantry regiments in the British Army. Hadn't anyone thought to check how much of the army was made up of Scots—especially the special regiments, the Special Boat Service and the Special Air Service? It would take them years to get back up to strength.

What they're doing is not patriotism, it's treason! he thought. Of course, many of them had disappeared with weapons and equipment: explosives, grenade launchers, machine guns and even a couple of American .50 calibre sniper rifles. In the right hands, those things could take out a soldier at over a mile away.

He mulled over the situation. He wasn't too worried about the desertions in the regular army, but some of the men who'd left the special regiments, particularly the SAS and SBS, were highly trained and unbelievably dangerous—so dangerous he never really trusted them. And they had taken weapons with them. They never really integrated with the regular troops, they seemed to think their shit smelled better than anyone else's. He knew many of them and they were not evil men, they just exercised deadly proficiency at their chosen vocation of delivering death to the enemy, on command. That made them both dangerous and unpredictable in this situation because they would now consider *him* their enemy. But who would be giving them their orders? Anyone?

The crowd stayed well back from the soldiers and APCs. The weaponry on show atop the vehicles seemed to have a sobering effect on many, though the noise continued, the chanting and yelling making his men's voices hard to hear on the radio.

The General fiddled with his sidearm, fingers twitching, feeling nervous and exposed. *Where are the police? Why isn't this crowd under control?* Then he saw the police standing with the protesters, looking straight at him, arms folded, and he understood.

Well, we'll just see about this, the bloody jocks. You can't just dissolve a country.

His staff car came to a stop in the car park atop The Mound where he intended to make his provisional command post. He emerged from his staff car, every inch an aristocratic military officer, looking for his combat commanders and was momentarily blinded by lights coming off television cameras.

"Get back you idiots! Move!" he yelled as a severe-looking female reporter thrust a microphone in his face yelling a question he couldn't hear over the din of protestors and screaming reporters. "Are you insane?" he yelled at close range into her face as he moved to join the officers. The reporter flinched away at first, but she'd reported from Iraq and Afghanistan and it took a lot to put her off. She chased after the general, microphone outstretched to try to catch his words.

"Right, we've been through this scenario. These are civilians and we're not expecting trouble—but tell your men to stay alert. Our orders are to occupy the building and arrest each and every Minister of the Scottish Parliament present. Then we are to transport them in the APCs back to the airport. Move with deliberate haste, get it done and let's get our arses home!"

Scottish Highlands, near future

Liz McColl sat and wept alone in her lounge. She wept for Scotland and she wept for her son Fin. Her telly showed the scene in town with all the protestors, helicopters and cameras.

She knew that he'd left his Regiment of course. She'd seen the news reports saying that nearly every Scot had deserted the British armed forces as soon as the Scottish Parliament had declared independence and Westminster had refused to recognise it.

The television showed the crowds on Princes Street and in the Gardens and up and down the Royal Mile, chanting and carrying banners demanding that the British Army go home.

Bloody English and their bloody pride! Why couldn't they just go home and leave Scotland alone?

More tears traced her red cheeks as the cameras showed the heavily armoured vehicles moving down Princes Street with their ominous camouflage paint, bristled with guns. Men in helmets and goggles poked out from top hatches, machine guns and rifles ready as they watched the crowds warily.

The scene jumped to inside the Parliament building where the entire Scottish Parliament sat, arms folded, faces defiant, as Gregor McAdam, Leader of the Scottish Independence Party and First Minister of Scotland, addressed them.

"So honourable members, colleagues, friends, it has come to this. Westminster has decided to send in troops and arrest us all . . .

"I say let them come!"

As his voiced boomed through the chamber and out of the TV speakers the chamber exploded into deafening cheering, every member standing and clapping, many with raised fists.

Liz wept harder, both with pride and fear, her breath now coming in ragged sobs.

She knew her son was out there, somewhere. He had disappeared with his large duffle bag a few days ago.

"Dinnae worry mum, I'll be fine. Everything will be fine. I love you. Dinnae worry." And he'd kissed her cheek and driven away.

She'd been so proud when he'd come back from Iraq and Afghanistan with all his medals and commendations. Of course, he couldn't tell her what they were for, but there they were on her mantle, next to his father's. All she knew was that he was a specialist of some sort in an elite regiment. She'd thought it was SAS but he'd never said, just shrugged and said he took orders for a living.

The TV cut to a scene outside as soldiers began spilling out of the vehicles and surrounding the building, then switched to a shot of an aristocratic-looking man in army fatigues getting out of a heavy armoured vehicle of some sort. He swatted away a microphone held out by a female reporter, the BBC Scotland's political reporter, who'd been talking to the cameras just a few minutes before. Liz sniffed a bit at the woman's dress sense; she looked more like a prostitute than a reporter to Liz's eye, shameful.

The officer started yelling at reporters to get back in a voice used to being heeded and stomped away towards another group of officers, trailed by a herd of reporters shouting questions. Then, as he stood talking to some other army men, it seemed as if the entire head of a man in the background simply exploded into a red mist. His headless body crumpled lifeless to the ground, as the same thing happened to one of the other army men nearby and then another and another.

Then the TV picked up the sharp heavy crack of rifle shots, cutting through everything else. The scene on the camera blurred into swipes of colour and light. The silence following the rifle shots ended as women started screaming, everyone started running and the soldiers took cover, cocking their weapons.

Liz put her face in her hands, shoulders wracked with sobs, knowing her boy was there and that life would never be the same again.

Holy Shit Sunday

Camp Bastion, Afghanistan, present day

Utter chaos enveloped the massive hangar that served as the SAS operating base in a secure corner of Camp Bastion, Afghanistan. Around thirty bearded, wild-looking men shared the space with vehicles, weapons, ammo boxes and piles of military kit of all kinds. Heavy metal music echoed through the chamber. The hangar door stood wide open into the Afghan sunshine and the thundering noise of transports and helicopters periodically blotted out all attempts at speech.

No one had on exactly the 'regulation' uniform, which pissed off the REMFs, rear echelon motherfuckers. The scruffy looking men appeared to spend most of their time trotting around the hanger, stealing each other's stuff, eating each other's food and generally taking the piss. Everyone carried some sort of spoon, some wooden, some metal, some homemade, others obviously part of a silver collection that had been 'liberated' from one of Saddam's palaces during the initial invasion of Iraq. They used this to sample whatever anyone else was cooking, invited or otherwise.

The snipers, explosives guys and the Counter Revolution Wing guys held a corner to themselves. Birt and Fin sat on a tarpaulin they had spread on the concrete floor stripping their rifles, taking nips out of a canteen filled with Famous Grouse. They had barricaded off a small section of floor with crates and a Lando.

Fin spoke first. "Fuck."

"Aye."

It hadn't been a nice day. They had got in a messy contact with some Talibs and had to shoot their way out without air cover when their radio broke down. Again.

Fin fell back into silence as he vigorously brushed out the copper and burnt gunpowder deposits in his rifle bore, then threw down the cleaning rod. He paused a bit, then looked up, "You know Birt, you almost didn't suck today."

Sabjirt 'Birt' Singhe looked briefly surprised and taken aback. Praise wasn't something he'd ever heard from Fin, this sounded as close as he was likely to get. "Don't go soft on me pal. I ain't gonna fuck ya, nae matter how sweet you talk."

Fin laughed at that, dispelling the sombre mood for a moment, "Ha! Like I'd fuck a skinny little arseless shite like you."

"Here's tae my skinny arse then, keeping me safe from the likes of you." They shared another nip of Grouse.

Birt held the canteen up, "If me dad knew I was drinkin', oh mate, me life would nae be worth living."

"Sikhs don't drink?"

"Not supposed tae. Everyone I know does though."

Fin was starting to feel the whisky and began to feel morose and a bit angry. Birt didn't know what to make of it. Drink normally just pasted a grin on him and he started buying everyone rounds.

"My dad died when I was a kid."

Birt kept his peace. Fin had never offered much in the way of personal information before.

"He was a sniper too you know. Died in the Falklands," Fin continued and then took another nip off the rapidly emptying canteen. "It was that same cunt you know, Trentworth, what killed him. Remember that fuck from Iraq that killed all those women?" referring to their new theatre commander, now in charge of all British forces in Afghanistan.

Birt's head snapped up from the rifle bolt he was polishing, "Eh?"

"Trentworth. He was my dad's platoon commander in the Falklands, a Second Lieutenant or some shite. The way I heard it, he thought the war was gonnae miss him by. So the night before the Argies were gonna surrender he takes his platoon, right. They head off to take this so-called important objective, some meaningless patch of rock. He pretended he hadn't got the order to pause. That's what I found out anyway."

He shot another slug of whisky down his throat.

"The stupid bastard ran my dad's unit right into an ambush and then the fucker panicked, just like he did back in Basra. Lost his fucking head and called a retreat, right. My dad stayed behind and covered their backsides with just his sniper rifle. Six of our boys got the good news in the back as they ran, but the rest made it. We got his body back after the surrender. It had like 40 holes in it and someone had kicked in his face."

Birt picked up the canteen, then turned it upside down, one lonely drop fell out.

A roar in the background pulled their attention to the centre of the hanger. A twenty-five-a-side football match had spontaneously erupted. The field of play seemed to encompass most of the hangar with nowhere actually out-of-bounds.

Birt had a sudden thought, "Wait a minute, that was *your* dad? I've heard of him! McColl, as in Lachlan McColl VC? Guy that won a Victoria Cross?"

"Yeah well. It came a little late for him to enjoy it. I'd just as soon they'd kept their fuckin' medal and left me my dad. Doesn't seem a fair exchange," Fin spat out, then looked up at Birt, "How'd you know about that?"

Birt looked a bit embarrassed, "I know all the Victoria Cross winners mate. We have three in my family, Crimea, South Africa and Burma, fighting for the British Army".

"No shit?"

"No shit."

Feeling a bit worse for wear, Birt and Fin stumbled into the mess tent the next morning in search of a cure for their aching heads. The tent was quiet, with only a smattering of occupants, mostly Royal Marines by the look of them. Fin thought that their tense faces and early breakfast meant they were dialling up for a mission, probably that night.

Jimmy McLeod had chummed along with them, a grizzled explosives specialist who rarely shaved and managed to look 50, despite having barely passed his thirtieth. He didn't say much, but had adopted Fin and Birt as fellow Scots. Snipers and bomb guys tended to hang together, unified in their uniquely independent ways.

"You chaps ever have a wank after a contact?" Jimmy said.

Neither Birt nor Fin chose to answer, but some squaddie walking in front of them heard them and dared to speak up. "You guys do that too? Mate after a contact I just can't fucking help it. Three times yesterday, one after another, bang bang bang."

"Who the fuck asked you ya fucking wanker. Piss off."

As they ambled towards the end of the queue, Fin looked mournfully at Birt, "Why'd you make me drink all that whisky ya bastard?"

Birt gave his usual wide smile, not giving any hint that he felt the effects of their hard drinking session, "Yeah and yer mum loves it too."

"Gimme everythin' mate. Load me up," Birt told the contractor behind the counter. They called the catering staff 'Andy Capp's Commandos', after their acronym of ACC, which stood for Army Catering Corp. The running joke was that the catering staff had killed more soldiers than the rest of the army combined, hence 'Andy Capp Commandos'.

"Do Sikhs eat pork?" Jimmy asked. The Pakistani contractor scowled as he dished up the pork sausages and bacon.

"Definitely mate, definitely. Not beef though," Birt said, gazing appreciatively at the growing pile of eggs, bacon, sausage, beans, tomatoes, mushrooms, fried bread and hash browns as it accumulated on his tray.

"Cows are sacred, eh?"

"Yeah, somethin' like that pal."

"Hmm. No animal is sacred in Scotland, except maybe deer, but we still eat them."

"Aye, mate I sometimes eat Scottish cows. They're not sacred," Birt laughed.

They wandered back to find a table near a television in the corner where a few Marines sat watching the news.

The presenter sat in the bright coloured studio, with a large picture of the Edinburgh skyline in the background, "We now join Jeremy MacAvoy in Edinburgh where he has been reporting on the lead-up to the Scottish referendum. Jeremy are you there?"

The camera cut to a loud demonstration going on in front of the Scottish Parliament behind the reporter.

"Good morning Dermott, it has been an eventful few days in Edinburgh, and indeed London, as the reality sets in that the Scottish Independence Party looks set to win a historic landslide victory in the Referendum on Independence in just over a six weeks time."

At this Jimmy perked up and looked alive for the first time in days. Still, when he spoke it was just a terse, "Damned right."

Fin looked at Birt, "I didn't know about any of that, did you?"

"Yeah, I heard stuff, but we been kinda busy eh?"

The reporter continued, *"—Gregor McAdam promises that the Independence Party will seek separation talks with the British government within days if the referendum passes."*

The report cut to a scene of Gregor McAdam, the leader of the Scottish Independence Party delivering a speech, rallying the party faithful.

"Now is our time. The time for Scotland to take her rightful place as a full and free member of the family of nations. This is not about oil, it's not about the past, it's about the future. It's about Scotland's dignity and it's about Scotland's right to govern itself. But more than anything else, it's about Scotland's right to determine her own destiny."

The programme cut back to the talking head of Jeremy MacAvoy. *"Mr. McAdam's message of dignity and an independent destiny has struck a deep chord throughout*

Scotland, especially the western and northern regions, traditional centres of nationalist sentiment in Scotland. When the vote takes place, they expect to voice their opinion loud and clear. Back to you Dermott."

Jimmy's eyes were blazing now and he had a smirk on his face. Again, under his breath he growled, "Damned fucking right we will."

Birt nudged Fin. "What do ya think then, eh?"

"Don't know. Never thought about it much."

Jimmy had started to get himself worked up.

"Come on, pal, independence. Freedom. A real country . . . No fucking plonkers lording it over us anymore."

"What makes you think our plonkers would be any better than their plonkers? Anyway, you can't turn on the news most days without some Scot living in London telling us what they're going to do to Britain next. Seems like we're already in charge," Fin answered with a grin, enjoying winding up the usually silent Jimmy. Finally finding a chink in the explosives expert's armour was too good to pass up.

"Don't fuckin' matter. They're our fucking plonkers. If we fuck it up, then it's our fuck up. Better than having a bunch of English arseholes fucking it up for us!"

Jimmy looked to Birt for support, an unlikely source, but he suspected he knew how the Sikh would answer. He'd grown up around Scottish Sikhs back in Glasgow.

"What do you think Birt?"

"I was born in Scotland mate, grew up there. I might be a Sikh, but I'm Scottish Sikh. If we vote to be free, we should be free! Simple as that."

Jimmy clapped his hand on Birt's shoulder, "Well said pal, well said."

Fin lowered his voice, "What happens to the Army boys? If Scotland goes its own way, we might have some thinking to do. Seems like half the Special Forces are Scots!"

Birt held up a newspaper he'd been scanning, "Aye ... Says here London won't have it though, not with all the new oil they been findin'."

"And bloody fucking right, too, stupid jocks."

The sharp cockney voice came from a young, hard looking Royal Marine from a nearby table. His dusty uniform and haggard eyes told them he'd just come off stag (guard duty), which explained his crankiness.

"What the fuck is the fuckin' the point anyway? Ain't Scotland better off in the union?"

His harsh street accent drowned out all conversation at the tables near them and the hubbub died instantly. Everyone looked their way, smelling a fight.

Only a slight tic in his cheek betrayed how Jimmy felt at this unwanted interruption. But he smiled and in his best fatherly voice said, "If that's true pal, what the fuck is it to you?"

"I'm not your fucking pal, arsehole. Here's what I think, right. It's all about the fuckin' oil, right. Now you lot have found more oil you just want to keep it for yerselves."

Birt just grinned, eyes wide, but he started rubbing his chin, just like he always did before a fight.

"You ignorant fuckwit, didn't you just say Scotland would be worse off outside the UK?"

"Of course you would. Think about it like. Could Scotland afford an army of its own? Could you pay for all the stuff you need to run a country? Really, what would be the fucking point? It's just stupid. Why turn the clock back, no point. Complete fucking waste of time."

Jimmy kept on his fatherly smile, but he quietly and slowly pushed his chair back from the table as he started speaking again. Birt and Fin shifted subtly, readying themselves for action.

"Well then pal, why don't we all just turn everything over to Johnny foreigner over in Europe, or even the Americans and let them run everything, eh? We'd all be better off then, eh, if we don't need our own country."

This obvious wind up brought a rare smile to Fin's face, but the London boy took the bait.

"What a load of fuckin' shite. The Yanks are completely different to us. They talk different, act different, their government's completely different, what's it got to do with them?"

Fin looked over at the young fire-eating commando for the first time, taking in his solid frame and angular features. The young man sat back and folded his thickly muscled arms staring back at Jimmy and his little party, not impressed with the scruffy lot of them, not yet catching on to who they were.

Jimmy pushed his chair back further and turned towards the marine and cocked his head, waiting for the idiot's brain to catch up to his mouth. It was a race his brain was never going to win. Finally Jimmy took a deep breath and in a quiet slow voice, addressed the young marine. Fin and Birt knew what was coming and shifted further, getting ready.

"Listen you ignorant little twat. You dinnae know the first fuckin' thing about it. Now piss off over to your bootneck cabbage head fuck-buddies over there in the corner and leave the real men alone to talk about grown up stuff, ya get me?

The burly marine growled and launched out of his chair straight at Jimmy, drawing back his fist as he came.

In a swift, catlike motion, Jimmy kicked up without leaving his chair, catching the young commando square in the face with the sole of his desert boot. The smashed nose gave a sickening crack. The Marine crumpled to the ground groaning, blood flowing from beneath the fingers he used to clutch his face.

Jimmy, Fin and Birt looked around and counted all the other Royal Marines in the mess—maybe ten of them—all on their feet, all staring back, hands balled into fists and jaws tight.

And then, all hell broke loose.

The residents of Camp Bastion, or indeed of every coalition base in every province of Afghanistan, always referred to Sundays as 'Holy Shit Sunday'. The Taliban prayed on Fridays, planned on Saturdays and mortared the camp on Sundays.

This Sunday proved no exception. Fin and Birt were coming to the end of a double stag they'd been dicked as punishment for their part in the melee in the Mess Hall. They'd sent three Marines to the hospital and damaged several more before being overwhelmed, just as the MPs waded in. Lachie, Major Lachland Sutherland, their CO, hadn't been impressed, but he'd covered their arses with the headshed. All they'd drawn was double stag. Their series of successful kill or capture missions in Task Force Black, a partnership with the US Delta Force, gave them a bit of leeway to 'let off steam' as Lachie had explained to the base commander and the Marine's Commanding Officer.

Fin just hoped that his name didn't reach the ears of Trentworth, their new shite arse theatre commander. Every time that bastard's name came to mind he broke into a sweat—not in fear, but in cold rage.

Something felt wrong today though. He recognised the feeling and it meant trouble. Holy Shit Sunday. Hot sand blew lazily around the anti-car-bomb barricades at the front gate, but no other sound disturbed the early morning silence. Usually, even at this hour, hawkers gathered outside the gates, ready to sell their wares to any coalition soldier who stepped outside the gate, from nasty Arab porn to the latest pirated DVDs. Not so today.

Birt, true to form, kept scanning the horizon from their reinforced sanger, hoping to spot the Sunday mortar crews before they started. His head ached from lack of sleep and his eyes ached worse from straining through his high-power spotting scope.

They both heard it at the same time, the hiss of an incoming mortar.

"Fuck! Get down!" Fin shouted at the grunts down on the gate below him. The sound told him everything he needed to know. Big mortar, headed right towards the gatehouse.

No sooner did he finish shouting than the mortar struck home, then another right after.

He clicked on his radio to shout the alert, hearing another hiss, this time coming his way.

Then everything went black.

Andy Skeen

Tartan Chess Master

Scottish Independence Party HQ, Edinburgh, Scotland, a few years ago

Gregor McAdam, Minister of the Scottish Parliament, closed the door to his parliamentary office, resisting the urge to slam it behind him. He stalked to his desk and sat down, staring bleakly at the leather blotter that lay there. Finally alone, where no one could see or hear him, Gregor suddenly started slamming his open hand down on the defenceless blotter in rabid frustration, "Fucking—ignorant—granny—amateur—fucking—dilettantes!"

The phone beeped once, interrupting this outburst, and the always-calm voice of his executive assistant Jean calmed him a bit, "You have a call Minister, it's the party sec."

He took a couple of deep breaths, "Thanks Jean, put him through."

The smooth Edinburgh accent of the SIP Party Secretary issued from the earpiece, "I know you're probably angry Gregor—"

"You're probably fucking right I'm probably fucking angry! I'm going to quit the party after this. This is a load of fucking shite and you fucking know it! We're never going to win the referendum like this Alistair, never. And it's the fault of a bunch of cardigan-wearing blue-rinse biddies with no fucking clue how to run a party or win a public vote. That bunch of fucking eejits spend more time trying to close independent schools and raise taxes than they do trying to win this country its freedom! This is the Independence Party, Alistair, not the Old-Fucking-Labour-Screw-The-Rich Party!" Gregor's anger and the clipped vowels of his broad Glaswegian accent contrasted strongly with the calm dour polish of the privately schooled Edinburgher Party Secretary.

"I know, I know, calm down Gregor and listen, I have some information for you, some new polling data … "

"Fat lot of good polling data will do now that we're to have another boring do-nothing nobody as leader!"

"Oh, I think this just might."

"No one is going to vote for the referendum with that socialist old cow in charge and you know it! She doesn't really want independence, she wants to rule. She's just going through the motions."

"I know Gregor, just listen to me. There's a new ClearGov poll coming out tomorrow. Listen to this, the poll says an overwhelming majority of Scots would vote for 'Yes' on the referendum if the SIP publicly stated that its only function would be to hold a referendum on independence."

Gregor bolted upright in his chair, " … say again …"

"OK. They put in the field a poll which asked, 'if the SIP publicly stated that the party's only policy focus going forward would be to win a referendum on independence, after which it would disband as a party, would you be more or less inclined to vote for the referendum.' Listen to this, nearly 70% said they would be more inclined to vote 'Yes' if that were the case."

As the implications of that sunk in, an uncharacteristic smile replaced the Glaswegian MSP's signature scowl. Then he began spewing rapid-fire questions at his old friend, "Is the data good? Is it broad enough? Who put them up to it?"

"Slow down pal, slow down. One question at a time. Yes, it is good poll, with a large pool and a broad demographic cross-section from every parish in Scotland. It was my idea, but that's just between you and me. The 79ers would go mental if they knew I'd started this, and the whole thing would blow up in our faces. I've thought you were right from the beginning Gregor. Our message is obscured and no one trusts us to run an independent Scotland, and who can blame them really? Sean agrees. He put up the money for the poll and he thinks you should be the next leader. Now you have the ammunition. We need to get you ready to face the press immediately after releasing the poll. I'll schedule a press conference for you," Alistair said, his own excitement breaking into his normally dour voice.

"That is of course assuming that you'll be staying in the leadership contest after all," he then asked innocently.

Gregor let out a bark at that. The polling data had dispelled his anger completely. He had suddenly moved from a world of empty nothingness and inevitable decline, into a whole new realm of possibility and promise. After a lifetime of striving, he might achieve his dream, a dream of dignity and freedom for his beloved Scotland.

May Day 2007 had marked the 300th anniversary of the Acts of Union when Scotland sold out. Gregor thought he could now see the possibility that those Acts could finally be overturned and the vow made in the nearly 700 year old

Declaration of Arbroath finally fulfilled. 300 plus years of colonial whoredom, but now the beginning of a chess-like strategy began to form in his sharp political mind.

Alistair had certainly done his work well, calling in old favours, cajoling, entreating and convincing reporters from every major media outlet to come to a press conference. It helped that Sean had come of course.

Cameramen and still photographers vied for places in the front row of the Scottish Parliamentary pressroom as Gregor prepared to make his statement.

ClearGov had distributed its poll far and wide and Alistair had alerted them to its significance. Now Gregor had to follow up and close the deal.

"Good morning everyone, and thank you all for coming.

"By now you will have read the poll suggesting the Scots' desire for independence from the United Kingdom.

"It has come time for this party, my party, the party of Scotland, to heed their voice and change course.

"I am here today to call on the Scottish Independence Party to abandon the policy of attempting to assert itself as a governing party, and instead align itself with the goals and aspirations of the Scottish people. If I succeed to the leadership, I will recast this party as one with a single goal and no other—the rebuilding of the dignity, self-respect and independence of the Scottish people, emancipating the once-proud Scottish nation from the shackles of its colonial overlord."

The Scotsman
McAdam Wins SIP Leadership

Gregor McAdam was named leader of the Scottish Independence Party ahead of the next general election this autumn. If elected as First Minister, he has promised to hold a referendum within his first year of office and if it wins, to take Scotland out of the UK with or without the agreement of what he calls the "English government".

Polls are showing the SIP to be on track to win an overwhelming parliamentary majority.

Andy Skeen

Fear and Greed on Thames

The Aberdeen Daily News
Petroflox to Operate Deep Water North Sea Oil Field Development

Petroflox, the international oil & gas facilities service provider, has today announced that its Resources division has increased its interest in several blocks in the North Sea. The blocks are generally thought to be untenable for exploration and production.

Petroflox Resources has acquired controlling a interest in several smaller companies, including Liguria Energy (Craigleith) Limited, and agreed to purchase the interests of three other partners, giving it complete control of a huge swathe of unexploited deep-sea oil fields.

James McManus, Group Chief Executive, commented, "With these changes to the field ownership and our role as operator, we believe we are in a better position to assess the viability of this previously abandoned untapped asset."

The Craigleith field is believed to have vast quantities of oil, equal to, or greater than, the entire amount that has been extracted from the North Sea since drilling began.

However, the depth of ocean, and thickness of the ocean floor on top of the field meant that it had previously been considered unrecoverable. Some industry experts think that Petroflox's pioneering remote-operated deep-sea underwater drilling robots, with new flexible high-pressure pipe technology, puts the oil within reach.

Jeffery Chambers of the Petroleum Research Unit said, "If Petroflox can realise the full potential of the blocks, the decline of British North Sea oil will be reversed for decades to come, potentially making Britain self-sufficient in oil and natural gas."

London, England, present day.

Cold sweat pushed its way onto Prime Minister William Gordon's upper lip. He could feel it gathering in his armpits and soaking through his shirt. He nonchalantly wiped his lip with a tissue, pretending to blow his nose. He couldn't let any of his team of advisers see his weakness.

The Scottish Independence Party was going to win its referendum, and win it easily. It hadn't taken long for his politician's mind, a mind constantly calculating the nature of gaining and holding power, to figure out what that meant. The SIP would try to take Scotland out of the Union. If they succeeded, he would no longer be Prime Minister, pure and simple.

He had a stark choice: political oblivion or fight to hold the Union together … and keep his job. That would be the right thing, both for himself, and the Union. A unified Great Britain commanded more wealth, potential and stability than a divided one ever could.

The elephant in the room was the oil of course. They simply could not let the oil rights go to Scotland. It would bankrupt the government in lost tax revenues and cripple the economy.

He decided to focus on those issues. He cut away from the ugly thought that his motives weren't pure, that he maybe he just didn't want to be a 'nobody' again. He was one of the most powerful men in the world, effectively in control of the one of the world's largest economies, with a nuclear arsenal and a place at the highest tables of world diplomacy.

If he lost this fight he would just be a fat ugly northerner. The type of women he liked, young women who were attracted to power, would spurn him once again. He would be consigned to the dustbin of political history – a short-serving PM who had never won an election on his own merits, wasting away the rest of his life playing golf. Or worse yet, he would have to spend time with his bitter nag of a wife.

Sweat dripped off his face now, and he had started struggling to breathe as his thought process took him to those dark thoughts. But he hadn't got where he was panicking and he got hold of himself quickly. Not for him that path. He would fight. He must fight. It really was the best for the nation surely. All of the nationalist rubbish was a backward step surely …

"Prime Minister?"

"Yes? What?"

"The press had these numbers yesterday, they'll be banging on the door for your comments …"

"Yes, they would be," the PM replied.

His newly appointed Director of News, Zoë Chandler, handled the press so skilfully she seemed made for the job. Just the day before she'd made a BBC correspondent look like a bumbling idiot. "Yes James, the economic forecasts that were the basis of the revenue projections were wrong, which means this budget will not balance. But as you also know, this Prime Minister was not responsible for this budget or these predictions. What should we do James, cut funding for the NHS or perhaps reallocate funds from the BBC's inflated TV licence fees?"

It might backfire of course. The reporter would be out for blood, but she could handle the press.

The PM wished she wouldn't interrupt him when he was thinking though. Her speed of thought and reaction made her extraordinarily impatient. Still, she had great legs and the way her expensive trouser suits clung to her taut athletic buttocks brightened his day. She'd even indicated her availability, something he would have to consider more deeply.

"Tell them this is a democratic country and that this government supports all the regional assemblies. But, it is the stated policy of this government that no devolved government may unilaterally hold a referendum. If such a referendum were held, it would probably be illegal. It is also the stated policy of this government that the United Kingdom shall remain whole, sovereign and democratic with the Westminster government at its heart—"

Zoë replied immediately without letting him finish speaking, "Should we take such a strong stand so early Prime Minister?" She'd seen this in him before, his strength and reckless decisiveness. It was one of the things that made him sexy, in a rough working-class sort of way. To Oxford-educated Zoë, it differentiated him sharply from the cynical Oxbridge neuters she often found in her company. Still, she thought, this time we really should tread softly.

"Yes we should. We may not be able to keep the SIP from winning the referendum, but we may keep them from taking rash action. We can throw them a carrot, more fiscal autonomy perhaps, within EU constraints and still under the Bank of England, but that's it."

"And the electoral issues Prime Minister? They'll say you're simply being venal, trying to hang onto power." Zoë asked intently, "What do I say to that?"

He stalled for time, "Isn't this what I pay you for dear?"

This is where things get complicated, the PM thought. For nearly a decade now the seemingly overwhelming Labour majority depended on the staunch support of the blindly loyal Scottish Labour electorate. Take out the Scot parishes now and Labour would be in a minority to a resurgent Tory Party—a party finally putting its old class elitism aside and beginning to grasp back large portions of the muddled middle ground vote from Labour.

Presenting this issue in the press would take some finesse.

"Deny it completely," the Deputy Prime Minister said suddenly from his chair a few metres away, where he had been busily swilling coffee and eating pastry, "It's got nothing to do with that and everything to do with your duty to King and Country to protect and preserve our lawful and democratic institutions. We have to take the high moral tone on this, Prime Minister. If we don't we'll be made to look like the bad guys when all we're trying to do is what's best for the country."

The PM considered.

"What would happen if we suspended the Scottish Parliament?"

Zoë shivered in her Jimmy Choos, with the excitement of finally being at the centre of Government policy. She didn't notice how the PM's hands shook a bit, or that he was sweating. He'd never seemed so resolute or powerful to her, a solid presence at the end of the table, making decisive and nation-changing decisions.

"Think about that everyone and we will reconvene this afternoon. I'm sorry, I have another meeting to attend."

The representatives from Petroflox had been waiting for 15 minutes in a Number 10 meeting room when Prime Minister William Gordon swept into the room with the Secretaries of State for Environment, Energy and Scotland in tow. The Prime Minister appraised them a single glance, highly polished and groomed, expensive suits and watches. None of those measures could entirely hide their working class Scottish origins, however. Something about their features gave it away. The PM unconsciously let his accent slip back to his own working class roots.

"Gentleman, sorry to have kept you, this morning's cabinet meeting ran over."

The CEO of Petroflox and his head of Engineering and Geology stood as they entered, "Quite all right Mr. Prime Minister, I hope we're not taking you away from anything critical."

"Nothing that can't wait a little while Mr. McManus. What can I do for you?"

"Well, I'm sure you've been briefed on recent developments in the North Sea oil fields and my company's new technologies—"

"Only in the most general terms Mr. McManus, I haven't had time to read the report in detail."

"Yes sir, I prepared this summary for you in case that might be the case. I know you are terribly busy," he said passing over a single sheet of paper. "The press is not exaggerating the potential of the fields Prime Minister. If anything, they are understating them. We're estimating that our blocks alone have the potential to double current output within five years."

The PM kicked himself for not having paid more attention to his briefing from his Energy Secretary. But what did they want from him?

"That sounds like wonderful news to me. Do you need something from His Majesty's Government to make it happen?"

"No sir, not at all. The current tax, incentive and subsidy regime your Government has put in place for North Sea exploration and production is one of the things that makes possible what we and our consortium partners are doing," he paused.

"Well, what is it Mr. McManus?"

"We, that is, Petroflox and our consortium partners, are deeply concerned about the political situation in Scotland."

"That makes two of us Mr. McManus," the Prime Minister replied, immediately regretting the flippant remark.

"Yes sir. Please have a look at the section that relates to the tax generating potential of the find over five, ten and fifteen years Prime Minister."

The PM scanned to the section and began to read. The numbers were indeed huge. So huge in fact, that he felt his heart rate begin to rise. He didn't say anything, but let the silence build. He still didn't know what this was about, but the obvious ramifications for the economy of the United Kingdom should those revenues go to Scotland instead, were immediately obvious.

"Prime Minister, no doubt you've heard that the SIP have declared that they will disband their party as soon as independence is achieved and melt into the other political parties—"

The Scottish Secretary butted in. Scottish politics was supposed to be his responsibility so he felt the need to contribute. He also thought he would remind his rivals at the table of his close relationship with the Prime Minister by using his first name, "That's true William, and all indications are that they mean it."

"Yes sir, they do. Many SIP politicians have already begun to declare their future affiliations with the other three main parties, or one of the fringe parties. We've done the analysis on the future makeup of the Scottish Parliament and conclude that it will be unfavourable to both business generally and the oil industry specifically. If Scotland gains its political independence and takes control of the North Sea in the current political climate, we believe that the oil fields will not be economically viable."

"In other words, you'll be out of business."

"In other words, sir, the massive oil and natural gas deposits will probably stay in the ground while a Scottish Parliament, ruled by a coalition of environmentalist and socialist-leaning parties, twiddles its thumbs and argues about whether or not it should have a military or nationalise the banking industry."

Smart, he thought. They're here to fight for their cash cow, but their argument focused solely on what was good for both Scotland and the United Kingdom.

"I understand all this gentlemen. What do you want me to do about it?"

"Sir, we believe you must keep the United Kingdom together at all costs. Or, if independence is a foregone conclusion, you must keep control of the oil rights."

Again he paused to think. He couldn't be seen to be taking orders from the oil industry in front of his cabinet colleagues. "I will take your comments under advisement gentlemen," he replied and got up abruptly and left the room.

The stench from the body next to him forced him to take shallow breaths and keep his head turned away in disgust.

Saville Row Suit, Jermyn Street shirt and tie and still the man exuded rank wafts of foulness—the smell of nervous sweat, cigarette smoke and the type of halitosis that indicates a slowly rotting, virtually pickled liver, mingled with the musty metallic smell of the Commons chamber. Still, the man supported him wholeheartedly, ensuring he won the leadership contest. Putting up with the smell he exuded was a small price to pay for becoming PM.

The bright lights and stuffy air of the debating chamber contributed to the Prime Minister's discomfort as he prepared for his first commons speech since assuming power.

He wanted to focus on reform and investment, but he knew what the topic would be when Question Time began. His opening gambit would be an attempt at a pre-emptive strike.

"Order, order, the speaker recognises the Prime Minister."

The benches behind him erupted into raucous cheering, those opposite answered with bitter guffaws and a few hisses. The last election had been bruising for both sides and the parties across the way were more than normally bitter and angry.

It took several minutes for the speaker to bring order to the commotion as the backbenchers behind him stood to welcome themselves back to power.

"Order! Order! The honourable members of this esteemed house are reminded that decorum will be maintained at all times and that we will not tolerate these outbursts!

"Again the Chair recognises the Prime Minister, William Gordon."

The new Prime Minister stood slowly and took a deep breath, smiling as he received the more muted applause of his backbenchers.

"Previous governments," he began, bringing laughter from behind him and angry muttering from across the chamber, "had negotiated with the countries that make up the United Kingdom in good faith and in the interests of democracy and self-determination, to devolve certain powers to regional assemblies. I believed in devolution then, as did my party.

"Since that time, the creation of bloated and unpopular bureaucracies in Wales and Scotland has squandered billions in public funds at a time of economic and international uncertainty, increasing crime and eroding standards of healthcare and education across the country.

"This money could have been used to improve public services and bolster law enforcement and military effectiveness to support our brave soldiers overseas, instead of lining the pockets of politicians and bureaucrats in Edinburgh and Cardiff that are often a laughing stock even among their own constituencies.

"The negotiated devolution of certain powers from Westminster to the regional assemblies was made on the explicit understanding that the central government would retain sovereignty, and that full independence was not part of the settlement, nor would it ever be.

"Honourable members and colleagues, I assert to you that Britain has room and need for only two levels of government, the national and the local. Devolution to regional assemblies has proven itself to be an abject failure. The assemblies themselves are pointless talking shops that have become the haven of radicals and extremists pushing outdated and self-destructive ideologies."

The SIP members had already begun to shout, forcing the speaker to bang his gavel yet again. The shouting quieted, but a mix of excited approval and angry defiance stirred the chamber and refused to die away.

"Under no circumstances should we allow the economies or civil administration of the United Kingdom to be cut down or diminished. The whole is infinitely greater than the sum of its parts and benefits every person in every part of the United Kingdom. That is why we are launching a consultation on the effectiveness of the regional assemblies with the question on their future remaining fully open."

The Times
Government Calls Time on Regional Assemblies

The government today announced a review of effectiveness of the Scottish, Welsh and Northern Ireland regional assemblies. On the surface, this is being touted as a way to settle any outstanding questions left when the regional assemblies were formed. Behind the scenes however, ministers are saying that this government intends to trim the sails of the assemblies, or even dissolve them, in light of the developing situation in Scotland, which threatens to tear the United Kingdom apart.

The leaders of each regional assembly vowed to take every lawful measure necessary to protect what they see as their "national rights". Gregor McAdam, the newly elected First Minister of Scotland and head of the Scottish Independence Party, went one step further, claiming that any attempt to dissolve the Scottish Parliament would result in Scotland unilaterally seceding from the United Kingdom.

Andy Skeen

Tango in the Sand

Near Basra, Iraq, March 2003

Two commandos rolled off the inflatable raft and eased themselves into the reeds at the side of the Euphrates River. The raft carried on as if nothing had happened, the remaining men alert to the sound of AK fire and explosions in the distance.

They pushed to the edge of the reed bed, then stopped to check their location through their night vision. Satisfied that they were alone, they checked their weapons and equipment to ensure no moisture had got in, especially the big sniper rifle one of them carried. They began their silent trek to their designated Observation Point about 500 metres from the water's edge.

"What they saying on the net?" Fin asked.

Blowing sand filled the view of his sniper scope as it searched the murky early morning landscape. Shamal winds had taken sand five kilometres into the sky. Dawn would be coming late today.

"No air cover mate, fly boys are all up north with the Yanks, giving the good news to some sorry cunt who pissed in their porridge. No one will fly in this shit anyway," Birt shot back in a snappy Glaswegian drawl.

A piercing snap of light signalled that the lightning had started. Fin immediately began counting and barely got to one before the thunderclap shook the ground. Too close. He started to wonder if his rifle would act as a lightening rod in this weather.

Dawn had not yet begun to break over Basra. The two-man sniper team had dug into a shallow camouflaged foxhole. Fin McColl held a heavy, menacing sniper rifle, tucked into his shoulder.

Average size, dark hair, weathered rugged features with brooding, piercing eyes that rarely saw a smile. If you saw Fin without the combat fatigues and desert sniper suit, you would never suspect that he was one of the British military's most respected and infamous snipers. Special forces guys respected him, common soldiers revered him, but terrorists and militia in lots of other places, like Northern Ireland, feared and despised him.

Birt strained through the murk with a spotting scope. He looked a bit like a muscular version of cricket legend Monty Panesar. Rather than a turban, he had tightly wrapped his waist-length hair in a camouflage bandana. As a Sikh he was allowed a beard, but he kept it tightly trimmed and shaped in a jaunty style.

"It's too light for night vision, but we cannae see shit in this sandstorm," Fin whinged. "Now we got no fuckin' air cover. If those boys in Najaf come this way it could be an interesting fuckin' day."

The pompous visage of Col. Edward Trentworth pored over tactical maps of southern Iraq. Junior officers and aides rushed about, bringing messages, tending computer monitors, radios and dodging around the field command HQ.

"Well, I guess we'll now see what your Special Regiment *cowboys* can do Major. The only thing between the enemy and us is your men. Brief me on their status", he asked the stern man standing quietly nearby.

Without knowing it, or knowing why, everyone in the room unconsciously gave the unnaturally still, black-clad man a wide berth. No one looked at him, at least not directly. Some knew he was special, others just felt discomfited in the way that a prey animal senses danger in long grass by a watering hole. Every man and woman in the room was a professional soldier through and through. But they all knew this guy was the only real killer among them.

"Yes sir," the man said, his broad Highland accent rolling tightly across the 'R'. He leaned forward over the map table, using a pencil to indicate some specific points on the grid. His gnarled weathered hand and arm stretched out across the map pointing, a pert blond ensign noted a large round scar near his elbow that looked suspiciously like a bullet hole. To her, his grizzled features looked like a strange mix of bright-eyed movie star, Bedouin tribesman and Charles Manson … fascinating and terrifying.

"We used the waterway to insert the four, two-man sniper-observation teams. They moved covertly to their Forward Observation Posts, here, here, here and here. All four teams are now in place. The lynchpin is this team here, directly between Basra and our position near the bridge." The Major said, and then lowered his voice, "They're my best team sir, currently with the Counter Revolutionary Wing, Sergeants McColl and Singhe."

"CRW hmmm? Satan's Minions. Well, at least they won't have any qualms about killing." God he hated the so-called Special Forces, with their arrogance and lack of discipline. Now his life was in their hands. Instead of a ring of solid armour he had to trust his command to two bearded longhaired killers with nothing but small arms. It just added to his resentment at being left behind by the American 1st Marines. Imagine, a storied and decorated regiment like the 7th Armoured Brigade, the Desert Rats, guarding the backside of some snot nose American reserve division on a legendary drive on Baghdad. He should be in the spearhead. He deserved to be in the spearhead.

The Major seemed not to have heard the Colonel's scathing tone, "The teams are using suppressed .50 calibre sniper rifles we … ah … 'borrowed' from the Americans sir. It's a .50-calibre rifle with a range over two klicks—

Trentworth cut him off, impatient and condescending, "I'm familiar with the claimed capabilities of the rifle Major, thank you." He paused, then, "McColl you say? I had a McColl under my command in the Falklands. A Scot. Didn't much care for him. Bit of a maverick."

Special Forces field commander, Major 'Lachie' Sutherland stared blankly at the pompous windbag, containing his distaste only with a supreme effort. "Yes sir, I believe that was Staff Sergeant McColl's father."

Trentworth looked up sharply. "You don't say … "

Lachie suppressed a grin. He knew the story of Trentworth and Fin's father … and Fin's father's Victoria Cross. "They'll be fine sir. Those two are the best in the business."

"It's not them I'm worried about Major Sutherland." Trentworth turned to an attentive nearby aid, snapping, "Captain Jones, what's the status of your artillery?"

Officious and sycophantic, looking every inch like an accountant in a uniform, Jones visibly puffed up, "Sir, they are 'fire ready' and on the net sir," he answered, a bit too loudly.

"Good, we may be needing your services today."

Fin and Birt scoured the scene ahead, seeing only falling-down shacks and crumbling cement block buildings. Dawn was advancing, bringing a bit more light into their scopes.

Fin shifted, trying to ease his aching joints. Faint angry shouting carried on the sand-laden wind.

"They're up tae something Sarge," Birt whispered in a bad American accent, imitating the Americans he heard around Camp Doha before the invasion began.

"Stop calling me Sarge, ya twat. Radio it in, they're not trying for stealth. They might think the sandstorm is a good time to party in style."

"Roger that Sarge", Birt answered with a cheeky grin.

Fin loosened the bolt of the rifle an inch and checked for the tenth time that he had indeed chambered a round. He slammed the bolt home and flicked off the safety.

Birt stayed glued to his spotting scope, "Contact, ten o'clock." He paused, considering, "That's funny, looks like women, Shia women, wearing veils. Aren't the Shiites supposed to be on our side this week?"

Swinging his scope to ten o'clock, Fin could just make out a group of women, their distinctive black-veiled silhouettes outlined them easily in the gloom.

A sudden "phump" signalled that the insurgents had begun lobbing mortars.

"Mortars Birt! Call it in now! They're lobbing mortars back at the main force".

Birt clicked the switch on his headset, "Tango 7, Tango 7, this is Foxtrot 12. We have mortars firing from near our location. Take cover. We are unable to locate the firing points."

Through literally blind luck, the Iraqi mortar crew got pretty close to the command tents, knocking over equipment and shaking the ground.

Trentworth dove under the table, a look of sheer terror on his face, while Lachie stood impassively, arms folded and watched the chaos unfold around him. If they took a direct hit, being under a table wouldn't have made a damned bit of difference to how dead he would be. He noticed that the cute Ensign had ducked at the explosion, but stood up quickly. They shared a look and Lachie gave her a quick grin and nod. He respected her obvious grit and the look communicated their shared disdain of Colonel Trentworth.

Scottish Highlands, March, 2003

Liz McColl, mother of First Sergeant Finlay McColl, sat watching BBC coverage of the war in Iraq. She could hardly turn off the telly knowing that Fin was out there, her only child, and the only thing she had left in the world.

The reporter sounded upbeat, excited even. "We're going live now to Stephen Forest with the British forces somewhere near Basra."

The on-screen window showed the jerky pixilated view from a satellite telecamera. A reporter in blue helmet and flack jacket appeared in the midst of a dust storm. Liz could see some soldiers behind him huddled next to some military vehicles.

The reporter's voice sounded tired but very serious, "The sand storms are causing real problems here. Both the US and British commanders have halted their advance and are waiting out the storm. Supply convoys are all dead in their tracks, raising real fears of a logistical nightmare for the Americans further north. They've simply decided it's too dangerous to move in these conditions.

The correspondent paused, looking to his left, "Hang on a minute Dermott, something's happening, I might have to leave you …"

Liz saw that men were now standing or moving around behind the reporter.

The anchor in London said, "Stephen, we'll try to stay with you but make your safety the number one priority."

Liz heard a disembodied voice shouting, "Incoming! Incoming! Get down! GAS! GAS! GAS!"

The reporter on screen began fumbling with a gas mask but kept talking, "We've been told to take cover!"

A series of explosions shook the camera cutting him off.

"Bloody fucking HELL! That was close!" The man's fear had finally broken the surface and his normally smooth calm voice broke into high pitched screaming, "I think those are mortar rounds and they're coming very close, maybe a hundred metres away!"

The anchorman sounded even more excited, "Stephen's unit is obviously under attack, we'll stay with him as long as we can."

Liz held her breath as explosions grew louder. Then the telly's speaker registered the sound of distant automatic gunfire and the crack of bigger rifles.

Near Basra, Iraq, March 2003

Birt rubbed his whiskered chin with his thumb, "They're moving Fin, here they come!"

Fin settled smoothly into the big heavy black rifle pulling the stock firmly into his shoulder. He took a few deep steady breaths to calm his breathing, slow his heart rate and relax his muscles. He knew it was time to go to work.

The massive 20x powered scope brought the figures so close he could see terror in the eyes of the fifteen or so women marching directly at him just over a kilometre away. Behind them he caught glimpses of a squad of gunmen in civilian clothes. He couldn't get a good estimation of numbers as they all crouched behind the women, hiding like the cowards they were. But he did catch sight of their AK-47s and the menacing tubes of Rocket Propelled Grenades.

A terrified woman broke and ran for the cover of a nearby building. A fat, balding unwashed gunman traced the footsteps of the fleeing woman with a stream of fire, catching her back not ten steps into her run, ripping through her and throwing her to the ground where she laid completely unmoving.

This turned out to be poor decision-making on the gunman's part as his full torso came into Fin's view. As judge, jury and executioner, Fin skipped the jury deliberation phase of the trial and delivered his sentence with a half-inch lump of tungsten and copper.

The massive force generated by the slug pulverised the gunman's upper torso, picking his body up and flinging it away from the crowd in ragged bits of flesh and bone.

Birt reported, dead calm, "Hit."

The group, now barely 500 metres from the hide, stopped advancing and the women dove to the ground howling with fear. That presented Fin with more targets. A bearded Iraqi with a potbelly grabbed at a cringing woman and put a gun to her head as he dragged her to her feet. Fin again caressed the trigger keeping the scope on target through the recoil, sending another broken carcass cartwheeling through the air.

"Hit."

Another Iraqi, an officer, with a red headscarf and Saddam-style moustache, lashed out at a prostrate woman with his foot, pointing his AK at her huddled form, bellowing at her in fear and rage. Fin calmly engaged his third target, again riding the recoil.

Birt held to his spotting scope watching the action unfold, looking for threats and confirming kills. He watched as Moustache's body flipped end-over-end along the ground away from the woman. The round had blown off most of his shoulder and the left half of his rib cage.

Moustache's gun arm dropped to the ground, firing a few rounds as it fell, the dismembered fist clenching the trigger, falling amid the prostate bodies of dead militia and terrified helpless civilians.

"Hit."

No pause, no celebration, no remorse, Fin immediately began searching for new targets. They'd all gone to ground, hiding behind prostrate women.

The radio squawked into life again, "Foxtrot 12, Foxtrot 12 we can hear shooting up there, give us a sit rep! Do you have a fix on those bloody mortars?"

Birt clicked into his radio, "Contact front. We have a group of about twenty to thirty militia attempting to advance behind human shields, women. We have them pinned down, repeat, we have them pinned down."

"Roger that, get those mortars Foxtrot 12, they're finding their range!"

"Roger that Tango 7, as soon as you can arrange to switch off the sand storm for a minute we'll send every one of these mother fuckers to the virgins. Foxtrot 12 out."

Fin spared Birt a mirthless grin.

Back in the command tent Trentworth clenched his fists and jaw.

Mortar fire, human shields and low visibility ... all the ingredients of a complete fucking disaster. Trentworth turned to his aid, "Do we still have those BBC reporters embedded with us?"

"Yes sir."

"Fucking brilliant, Bolshevik Broadcast Co-op shite-head reporter, probably younger, and dumber than any of the fuckwit boys my daughter brings home."

Every male soldier within earshot had to suppress a smirk. Those that had seen pictures of said daughter knew she would have the pick of the litter.

"I hope those Special Regiment boys are as good as they think they are. The last thing we need is a blood bath live on national television. Tell them to get a fix on those fucking mortars and call in artillery, that's what they're there for, for fuck sake!"

"Tango 7, Tango 7, this is Foxtrot 12. Mortars launch, mortar launch, mortar launch, stay in your holes back there! We have civilians all over the place, call no fire, over!"

The combat controller squelched into his ear, "Roger that Foxtrot 12."

By that point, the gloom had slowly started to clear with the rising sun. Birt scanned the buildings and roadways. He finally spotted mortar teams in a street, "Got 'em. Two o'clock Fin, at two-five-eight-zero metres, wind steady from right at twenty-five, three-quarter value."

Fin scanned to two o'clock, catching sight of the mortar crews, watching as shells were brought forward and fed into the heavy mortars, then they adjusted the tube and loaded again. The militia had positioned human shields all around the site, bound hand and foot.

Birt flicked his collar mic again, "Tango 7 this is Foxtrot 12, we have them."

"Roger that Foxtrot 12, are they within range of your sniper, over?"

Birt glanced at Fin but knew the answer. Fin just grinned at him, "Roger that Tango 7, but we have no clear shot, over."

Trentworth glanced at Lachie, "Looks like your boys aren't as good as you thought Colonel. Get a grid reference Captain."

"Foxtrot 12, please relay the grid, over".

Birt gritted his teeth, he knew what was coming and didn't like it, "There's civilians all over, human shields. Call no fire Tango 7!"

Trentworth, still embarrassed at losing his cool, directed his anger at the sniper team, "Who the fuck do they think they are giving me orders? Typical," he said, glancing at Lachie, leaving no doubt that he meant typical of Special Forces. He chewed it over for a moment, then grabbed the mic from the Captain, "Foxtrot 12, this is Lt. Col. Trentworth, give me a grid reference immediately, or both of you will spend the rest of your time serving His Majesty by cleaning field latrines, do you copy that? Over."

Birt glanced at Fin's grim face and shrugged. Fin shrugged back with a nonchalance he didn't feel. Birt consulted his map, then studied the scene for a moment to determine the location,

"Roger that Tango 7, grid reference 524 100, repeat, 524 100. I repeat, we count at least 15 civilian human shields around the mortar positions. They're mostly women sir, over." No one answered him.

Fin kept to his scope looking for a shot, the view cleared briefly on one of the mortars and he fired, hitting one of the mortars, causing a small explosion. "I've got the range Birt, tell them I can do this!"

Birt clicked into his radio again, "Foxtrot 12, we have the range and have disabled one mortar, please hold your fire, hold your fire, over!"

A massive explosion shook the ground of the command tent, knocking things off shelves, blowing out the lights and causing general mayhem.

Somewhere in the distance someone howled in pain while one of his comrades yelled for help, "Medic! Man down! Man down!"

Trentworth gritted his teeth, "That's it, Captain, order the fire mission. I will take full responsibility. Fire for maximum effect. Get your snipers under cover Major."

Both the Geordie combat controller and Lachie answered simultaneously in nearly identical flat tones, "Yes sir".

Back in their hide, Fin and Birt heard the whistle of 105mm artillery shells flying in from over ten miles away, bringing in the good news to Iraqi mortar crews, as the artillery regiment began its barrage. They both pulled away from their scopes, not wanting to watch women and children die, sharing a look.

Trentworth had panicked again.

"Fin, those militia look ready to bolt! Left side, ten o'clock."

Fin jumped back onto the Barrett and swung onto the left of the huddled group of militia and their hostages trying to crawl back toward the edge of town. He spotted a leg with a combat boot exposed from behind one of the cringing women—tricky shot but it looked clear behind the leg. He settled into the rifle listening to his heartbeat and controlling his breathing.

The dust and recoil temporarily blinded Fin, but Birt watched the exposed militiaman's leg explode below the knee. Dust, blood and bits of flesh and bone erupted in a small plume where the man's leg had been, the boot and foot spinning off into the distance.

"Hit."

At that moment, the artillery shells began exploding where the mortar teams and civilian human shields were set up, blowing the entire area to pieces.

Fin and Birt could see the bodies of the human shields flying through the air as the first shells hit.

Scottish Highlands, March, 2003

The reporter had regained his calm, "The artillery nearby have opened up Dermott and we can hear distant explosions. The mortars have stopped completely. It looks like the army have the situation under control, but the sandstorms will continue to cause problems. Back to you in London."

Mrs. McColl could do nothing but chew her fingernails and wait.

Andy Skeen

Punjabi Rap and Lions Rampant

Royal Centre for Defence Medicine, Birmingham, England, present day

Fin was laid up in his bed, a stunned expression on his face as he watched the news on a tiny television in the corner of the crowded military hospital room, five bunks per wall. A young eager scouser in the next bed was bursting with something to say.

Private Tony Walcott had been the bane of Fin's existence since he'd been moved into the recovery ward at Selly Oak, to recover from his surgeries. The young soldier had figured out early that he was a 'blade', as the regular troops called members of the SAS Regiment.

"Sounds like this new guy's gonna sort tha' shit out, hey Staff?"

All the men in the room fell quiet, watching Fin warily to see how he would react to the young soldier's ill-conceived words. But Fin wouldn't rock the boat.

"Maybe so Tony, but he wants to take away something he has no right to take."

The soldier's pasty unshaven face coloured at the realisation that he might have offended his Special Forces idol.

"But Staff, yer no nationalist, I've heard you talkin', sayin' you don't give a shit about politics. I heard you complainin' about the Scottish Parliament being a waste 'o money and everythin'.

"Aye Tony, I have. But Scotland voted to have a Parliament and we have a right to it. This guy's got nae right tae try an block it."

The soldier swallowed, disappointed. "But he's been elected too! That's democracy too, innit? I just don't see the point of having three governments when one would do. The money could go to help people like, you know, like me ma back home, like."

Fin sighed. "Aye, you got a point. But Scotland won't put up with this. The Scottish Parliament might be useless, but it belongs to Scotland, all of Scotland, not just some fat bag of shite from Newcastle."

"But Staff, isn't it true that Scotland is better as part of the Union? Can they really afford to go it alone?"

"I don't know Private, but I do know what they call someone who sells themselves for money. They call them a whore."

Fin struggled to dress himself, and he noticed the movement had caused some blood to start seeping through the thick bandages covering the stitches on his shoulder.

He had politely declined the help of a nurse, but she couldn't help watching over him. She also couldn't help but notice his body, wincing at the various scars that told the story of an active Special Forces career. A few looked suspiciously like bullet wounds, others were knife slashes or cuts. He sported a large old ragged wound that had obviously been poorly sutured down his left thigh.

His doctor walked up, reading clipboard notes, harried and distracted, "Got your orders here Sergeant McColl. Immediate release. Eight weeks rest leave, what do you gents call it—up the line? Then report to your home unit for light duty. Odd, doesn't say what that unit is … "

The doctor paused as he considered the puzzle of an incomplete set of orders before he figured out what that meant. Certain secret deniable units rarely listed unit designations. He made the connection finally, "Ah … I see. Well, here's your treatment guidelines. Clean your wound daily and visit your local hospital once a week."

At that moment Birt burst into the room pushing a wheelchair, rapping in Punjabi to the music from his headphones that only he could hear. His singing was badly out of tune drawing winces from the medical staff, and groans and shouted complaints from the other soldiers on the ward.

Birt looked sharp in his civvies, all designer labels, gold watch and his beard groomed into a pencil thin outline. He even sported a Burberry turban. Fin considered this most amusing blend of cultures as Birt shot towards him, riding the wheelchair out of control, like a child riding a supermarket trolley, screeching to a stop and ramming his hospital bed.

The nurse held her tongue as the soldiers in the room all cheered and clapped and Birt took a wry bow.

"Mate! They told me to come pick up your corpse! And here ya are, movin' round and putting on … a really ugly shirt. You pick that out yourself?"

Fin couldn't hide how happy he was to see his mate, "What the hell are you doing here ya ugly fuck?" he asked, then, embarrassed, looked at the nurse, "Sorry Ma'am."

She smiled at his blush, "I hear much worse in here soldier, believe me," and turned to leave.

Birt gave the nurse his best 'I love you' smile, watching her shapely figure retreat from the ward.

The doctor cleared his throat, "Well, I take it this is your escort home? Good luck Staff Sergeant. Try not to come back again, OK?"

Fin laughed at the joke, saying, "Yes sir," since the doctor was also an officer.

Birt turned to Fin, "The Major's ordered me to drive ya home and look after you for few weeks. He's already told yer mum we're coming. Oh, he said something about making sure you didn't tear out your stitches."

Fin's face twisted into a wry grin, "Child-minder then."

"Aye something like that pal! What's yer mum look like anyway?"

"Me mum wouldn't be interested in a skinny fuck like you, I already told ya, but you might find a taker out in the sheep pen!"

This brought whoops of laughter from the other casualties as Birt pushed Fin from the ward.

England and Scotland, present day

Birt drove his funky boy-racer at breakneck speed all the way to Scotland, blasting out Punjabi rap, singing along, just happy to be alive. Fin was sure that Birt's sound system had done more damage to his hearing than all his years of firearms use combined.

They'd taken the A1 route through the east side of the country and stopped off three or four times at relatives of Birt's, although Fin couldn't unravel how everyone was related. They'd ended up eating a full meal each time, including some of the hottest but most wonderful curry he'd ever tasted.

At each stop, the women had served the men, then disappeared, only to clear the dishes and bring wonderful rice-based desserts and sweet hot tea. Some of the men he met wore turbans and beards, some didn't. Those without turbans sometimes served him alcohol, but not always. All of them treated him with incredible hospitality and respect, asking after his wounds and his time in Afghan and Iraq. He cottoned on quickly to the fact that Sikhs usually referred to all Moslems, no matter where they came from, as "Pakistanis", with unconcealed hostility.

His family's deep respect for Birt also became obvious. They showed him hundreds of photographs of Sikh men in British and Indian army uniforms and he started to understand Birt a little more, and why he served in the forces. The proud martial tradition of Birt's family came out strongly in those photographs. Fin also learned that one of the Sikh's greatest 'gurus' was a warrior and this high-caste Sikh family came directly from this warrior tradition. He even saw a Victoria Cross at a big house they stopped at in the Midlands somewhere.

The solid bond of mutual respect he shared with Birt, born of suffering and fighting together all over the world, grew over the trip as Fin truly began to grasp the great tradition that Birt represented. He found it not unlike his own family in many ways—generations of warriors, decades of selfless service, a tradition of excellence and quiet heroism.

He also found Birt's discomfort incredibly amusing, as many of the families they visited pointedly introduced young women to Birt, "this is such-and-such's daughter, you remember her …" Fin told himself to remember to ask Birt about Sikh marriage customs.

As they continued on their zigzag northern trek, he felt completely bloated and a little tipsy, but a feeling of contentment began to build the further he got from Hereford. He even found himself tapping his foot along with the crazy Punjabi rap, singing along with the English parts of the songs he'd heard ten or fifteen times by then.

He also feared for the future of his backside, knowing that as bad as the curry burned going in, it would be ten times as bad on the way out, which caused him to spontaneously start humming 'Ring of Fire' by Johnny Cash.

As they approached the border to Scotland they saw someone had put up a massive banner along the road. Just one word on it: FREEDOM.

Neither made a comment, Fin just raised his eyebrows.

As they approached Edinburgh, Fin finally persuaded Birt to turn down the music, "Let's go into town mate, see what's happening."

Driving through Edinburgh they saw signs and posters everywhere,

SCOTLAND WILL BE FREE

FREE SCOTLAND

LET SCOTLAND GO

YES TO INDEPENDENCE

GO HOME ENGLAND

Birt had decided to head to the Scottish Parliament just to see what was happening.

They couldn't believe what they saw. It looked like a protest-cum-street-carnival had been in operation there for weeks if not months. Fin also thought it looked like someone had carpet-bombed the place with Scottish flags, both Saltire and Lion Rampant.

They could only stare wide-eyed, mouths open as a constable waved them on, trying to keep the traffic moving.

As they crossed over the Forth Road Bridge that separated the Lothian counties from the Kingdom of Fife, and headed north towards the Highlands, the weather turned rainy and misty. They finally left civilisation behind when the road fell onto the wild expanse of Rannock Moor, a desolate empty landscape of deer, wild heather and sheep-eating bogs.

Bored with music, Fin had finally convinced Birt to let him listen to the news.

> "Welcome to JockTalk radio. The topic today is of course, the Referendum. In case you've been living in a rubbish bin and missed it, it's gonna pass and in a landslide. What's tae happen to Scotland? Gi' us your thoughts, just call 0800 JockTalk. First, let's hear from the head of the Scottish Independence Party, Gregor McAdam, recorded yesterday.

> "This nation has toiled under the yoke of colonialism for over three hundred years, since the greedy betrayal of the Treaty of Union. Now the people of Scotland will have the chance to speak. I hear them, their voices crying out for dignity.

> "We, their elected representatives, must move to affect their will, to allow Scotland to take its rightful place as an equal in the family of nations.

> "The Government in London thinks that our freedom is theirs to grant.

"It is not!

"Freedom is ours to declare, and we shall declare it!"

Scottish Highlands, present day

"Cup of tea … Sabjirt?"

"Oh, yes please Mrs. McColl, and call me Birt." He took to Fin's mother immediately. She reminded him of the women in his own family, kind and gentle on the outside with a spine of steel and not someone you would want to cross.

Liz McColl returned Birt's wide smile, "I'll just be a moment then. Oh, and please call me Liz. Fin, can you show Birt around? I've made up the spare room for him."

"Is it always so cold up here?" Birt asked as Liz bustled off to the kitchen to make tea. He couldn't help shivering a bit and welcomed the presence of the glorious coal fire popping and fizzing away on the hearth.

"Colder than Glasgow aye pal, always gets colder at night though. Have a look about, I'll be right back."

As life slowly returned to his legs and back, made numb from the long drive, Birt began to notice details of the room … a room which amounted to a shrine to various Scottish regiments and the action they had seen over the decades.

Old pictures—sepias, daguerreotypes and cracking old paper photographs—fought for space on the cluttered walls. Wild looking bearded men in military uniforms and kilts with feathered caps, brass button jackets and spats strutted across the walls, their strength and determination jumping out from the flat black and white images. Young men, serious hard-looking men, posing proudly in kilt uniforms carrying rifles, wearing chequered floppy berets or tight fitting caps. Photograph after photograph.

Pictures of proud men in kilts and tartan being reviewed by stern officers, and even members of the royal family. A jaunty parade of kilts marching under the Arc de Triomphe in 1945, all tassels, tartan and pride.

Birt did a double take on some of the photos of men that looked amazingly like Fin, like one of them had stepped out of those pictures and become Fin in this life. Each face betrayed immense pride, every stance bristled with confidence.

Old medals took pride of place, including a large collection next to a photograph of a stern looking man in a pith helmet and kilt, holding a long old-fashioned rifle with a long slender scope. Birt realised that he was probably looking at one of the earliest snipers in history, in Africa it said.

The eyes of the men were all the same. They burned bright and hot, but steady. No anger, no rage, just steel. Birt knew that look. He knew all of these men understood what it meant to kill. None felt remorse at the death they caused, but none felt pleasure in it either, only the satisfaction of a job done well. All had seen the faces of their targets close up in their scopes before they'd killed them. They were snipers, just like Fin and Birt.

He came to some old newspaper clippings, carefully mounted and framed. One caught his eye, LOCAL BOYS SHIP OUT TO FALKLANDS, which showed a picture of a soldier kissing his son, a stern-looking boy, maybe six years of age. Next to that hung a photograph of that same man, proud, with beret, a long sniper rifle slung over his shoulder looking off into the distance with the headline LOCAL MAN KILLED IN FALKLANDS. The subtitle read SURVIVED BY WIFE ELIZABETH AND SON FINLAY. Further along, another newspaper clipping read LACHIE MCCOLL AWARDED POSTHUMOUS VICTORIA CROSS.

One section of wall held more pictures of Fin's father, showing that he too practised the sniper's craft. There he stood, a stern slight-of-build Highlander, but tough and wiry like an old boot—just like his son. As he stared at the picture of the group of men standing with the CO something clicked in Birt's head— Trentworth. Trentworth had commanded Fin's father's platoon in the Falklands. Fin no doubt still held him responsible.

But not all the pictures on the walls were of military men. Some showed scenes of deer stalking in the Scottish Highlands, parties of aristocratic men and women wearing tweed with long old-fashioned telescopes, horses carrying deer carcasses, and even some of young Fin working as a ghillie, always in the background carrying a scoped rifle, always with his same serious expression. Birt recognised some of the aristocratic faces from the telly, but couldn't put a name to them.

Another section of wall showed wild downhill mountain biking pictures of crazy jumps and blurred speed. He smiled as he noticed the trophies and medals too, and a newspaper headline that screamed at him, LOCAL BOY SHOCKS PROS AT FORT WILLIAM DOWNHILL RACE!

Next to that he found one that read DEERSTALKER FOLLOWS FAMILY TRADITION, with the subtitle: FINLAY MCCOLL JOINS SAME REGIMENT AS HERO FATHER. It had two photographs, one of Fin in a kilted regimental uniform, another standing over a downed stag in the Highlands.

Moving along the wall to more recent photos he found the ones of Fin. He posed with a unit of men, all in black battle dress uniforms without any identifying markings on them. All the men smiled too wide, except Fin, which meant they must be

Americans. Birt remembered that Fin had cross-trained with US Delta Force for a six-month stint.

"Your tea Birt" She startled him from his inspection and he asked a question without thinking. "Who's this?" he asked, pointing at a picture of a stern looking man in an old colonial uniform who looked so much like Fin it spooked him a little.

"That's Fin's Great Uncle Hamish … he died in the Boer War, but … well … those are his decorations there," she said pointing. Birt had already noticed the Victoria Cross among Uncle Hamish's decorations. So, along with Fin's dad's VC and Uncle Hamish's, that's two in one family, a very rare thing indeed. They had that in common, the weight of tradition, the eyes of all his ancestors watching them, measuring their worth and their courage.

The men of this family had been Forces for untold generations … and snipers … and Highland Ghillies. Fin had the hunt in his blood, which is probably what made him such a natural sniper.

"All set, c'mon mate, finish your tea, it's music night at the pub."

Liz's eyes glowed, "Oona's been asking after you Fin."

Fin ignored her, but not Birt. "Oona aye? Who's she then?"

"None of your f'—", he stopped, looking at his mum, "sorry mum, mind your own business punk," he said with an embarrassed grin.

Birt snapped a cheeky salute, grinning at Mrs. McColl, "Roger that Sarge."

Scottish Highlands, 1994

Fin crept through the woods, his thumb on the safety of his Dad's beat up old service rifle, finger at the ready along the stock next to the trigger.

Bent at waist and knee, peering through the undergrowth to the sides and front, he moved slowly and methodically placing each step carefully, just as his Dad had taught him.

He'd just turned sixteen and he held a family heirloom, an American World War II era bolt-action rifle. The stock showed its age, but he'd aligned the sights at the old quarry and it shot straight as anything. It was tricky finding cartridges for the American .30-06 Springfield calibre, but his Uncle Hamish brought them to him from Dickson & McNaughton down in Edinburgh. "Now if you're out in the woods, and maybe you decide you need a deer or two for the family larder, pick up your bloody cases boy! Every gamekeeper for a hundred miles in every direction knows your dad used a .30-06 and no one else does. If they find a spent case, they'll come right to you and you know what that means eh?"

Fin drew a deep breath through his nose, smelling pine and the dank stench of deer musk. He thought he smelled a vixen nearby too. He knew the deer were close. He swept his eyes across the landscape taking in the distant snow-covered peaks of the surrounding Highlands and the lower pine forests where he knew deer waited.

Silently he wished he could spend all his life out here rather than in school. He hated school. The wind pushed through the pines around him, whispering to him, telling him to 'hush'. Yes, he would stay here all his life if he could, just like that American boy in that book 'My Side of the Mountain', who ran away and learned to live in the mountains, alone and free.

He thought he heard rustling in the bushes somewhere in front. Peering through his binos, he thought he spotted a patch of red-grey fur, a Red Deer in its dark brown-grey winter coat. He took some slow deep breaths to try and slow his heart and still his nerves. His heart pounded, he wanted this deer, and his family needed the meat. With his Dad dead, they struggled to survive on only his mother's War Widow's Pension. The pub down the road would buy any meat he didn't need. £1 per pound of venison was the going rate. Hard to beat that!

It took almost three hours to get the deer, a big fat hind, down off the hill and out of the forest in the dark. His old hill pony knew the way to the pub though, despite the darkness. He had no choice but to wait until dark, he couldn't afford a gamekeeper seeing him with a poached deer strapped to his pony.

He picked his way down off the hill, through the heather and around the granite sentinels that guarded the path along the gurgling burn that wound its way down to the Poacher's Pint. The pub's name never failed to bring a smirk to the young poacher's dark features, despite the fact that he'd never had a pint there, or anywhere.

Music and laughter seemed to seep out of the pub's walls and windows, spiking sharply louder anytime a smoker opened the door, or a kitchen hand emptied a bin.

He stuck his head into the kitchen at the back of the pub only to be confronted by the stern face of the publican's daughter. "What do you want then?" she demanded, sharp and challenging, as always. She'd been distant and tetchy since her mother, the publican's wife, had died in a car accident. Fin knew exactly what it felt like to lose a parent.

"Err … " he was struck speechless every time he saw Oona, "Ah … your Dad?" It never occurred to him that her manner towards him concealed exactly the same feelings.

Oona looked at him with wry suspicion, "Poaching deer again eh Finlay? Wait here, I'll get him."

He called after her, "The deer belong to no man, whatever the laird may say!"

"Oh aye? Tell it to the polis poacher boy!" she tossed her dark red hair, dismissing him as she went in search of her father.

A big rangy Highlander soon appeared at the back of the pub, grinning. He hadn't missed the flush on his daughter's face and knew immediately who was at the backdoor, "Ah Fin, what have ye then?" his sonorous voice boomed out into the dark. Fin always marvelled at the height of the man, and his wild untamed musician's waist-length hair.

"A nice heavy hind Mr. MacLean, perfect for stovies or stew!" Fin knew how to sell a deer carcass.

The publican looked over the deer, checking the condition of the meat, "Well shot son." Fin bristled at being called 'son', but it didn't show in the darkness. He would be a soldier soon, and the only man who had a right to call him 'son' was dead. "Right then, get it into the larder, I'll come weigh it."

Money was proffered and quickly disappeared into the boy's wool coat after they'd weighed the deer. "Tether your pony behind the larder and go into the kitchen then, I'll have Oona whip you up a stovie, you looks like you could use a good eat son."

Luckily the publican couldn't see Fin blushing furiously at the thought of having to face his daughter Oona, "Thanks all the same Mr. MacLean, I'll need to be getting home to me mum."

With that he picked up the lead of his pony and scooted off along the back trails that led to his mother's cottage, on an estate where as many generations of McColls had lived as far back as anyone cared to count.

Andy Skeen

Fiddles, flutes and freckles

Scottish Highlands, present day

Fiddle, flute and guitar wove a melodic tapestry with the sonorous voice of a dark rangy Highlander. He strutted among his audience, with a jaunty, exaggerated swing of his right forearm, snapping his fingers through the suspended eddies of dust and smoke.

'What a fucking cliché,' Fin thought, looking on a scene he'd witnessed since he was a boy, but with older, world-weary eyes. 'It looks like a fucking Visit Scotland advert in here.'

Fresh haggis stovies floated by, flaunting their contents with mouth-watering incense mixed with the sweet tang of well-kept ale. One of the musicians sparked up a pipe in the corner and the honeyed stench of hashish added itself to the mix, wrinkling Fin's nose. He wondered if this would make him fail his next drug test.

Stomping and clapping, the Highlander crooned of love lost, of meaning found, of places gone and friends far away. A Celtic flute, pressed to the plump pale lips of a melancholy ginger giant, chirped in with a sympathetic lament.

Fin delved into the newly arrived haggis and cheese stovie, a baked dish of haggis, potatoes and cheese, burning his tongue. He soothed the pain with the cold bitter balm of dark, rich ale, its fragrance and taste hinting of its remote North Sea island origin.

A roar erupted as the last refrain fell away. Sparkles of fine dust joined the smoke as the drunken and happy revellers stomped dusty, long-suffering floorboards and pounded uneven, pocked tabletops in ravenous appreciation.

A young woman emerged from the kitchen, wiping her hands on a discoloured bar towel and cast a shy smile around the pub, missing Fin, who steadfastly studied the head on his pint in a dark corner booth. She took her place in the corner and began lashing out an old Celtic melodic rhythm on the tinny, out-of-tune piano. All the instruments joined in, one by one.

Fin poured the last bit of froth from a tepid glass onto the top of a burgeoning frosty one. Tapping his foot he settled contentedly into the yielding embrace of cracked brown leather, trying not to stare at the piano player, who changed the pace with a seductive and haunting rhythm as backdrop to harps, flutes and fiddles around the room.

On first pass no one would call her beautiful, at least in the typical lads-mag sense. Her striking red hair fell in curly waves across slightly too-wide shoulders. A wee lump of baby fat bulged right where her bra strap stopped under her tight-fitting t-shirt. Too-pale skin, with heavy peppering of freckles on plump cheeks ... No, nothing about the girl said 'glamour queen'.

Fin rarely saw her face without a smile on it, except when he'd been deployed to Iraq the first time, or when the subject of her mother came up. And her deep green eyes somehow managed to blaze from her white freckled face, making his face burn every time they fell on him. Ever since he was twelve years old he'd been shrinking in shyness from that gaze. She terrified him more than Iraqi RPGs, more even than that sniper battle with the CIA-trained Afghan marksman. He usually managed no more than "Awright" whenever she spoke to him, at least in public.

A hand slapped him on his left shoulder sending a bolt of pain through his wound, "Awright Finlay my son?!"

Clamping down on the pain, Fin nodded as a grizzled wiry-framed man in corduroy trousers and a heather-coloured wool jumper slid into the booth next to him. "Aye pal, you?" he managed.

"Fuckin' brilliant now I'm here," the wizened geezer barked out, "been down south with the ferrets cleaning up some warrens. Kept back a bit o' beer money the missus don't need to know about," he said with a snort. "Pint?"

Fin just nodded and managed a tight smile. The pain in his shoulder from the man's greeting had nearly made him pass out and he still hadn't managed to clear his head.

"You don't look too good boy, what the fuck you doin' here anyway? Heard you was out killin' the Taliban or some other shite?" the old man said, his loud voice drawing disapproving stares from other drinkers. Fin slid down in his seat and pulled his cap down a bit further.

Fin opened his shirt a bit showing bandage, with the blood beginning to seep through again, just beneath his collarbone. The old man winced at the sight of the blood. Fin had a bigger bandage just above his left shoulder blade where the shrapnel had exited. Luckily it hadn't hit his shoulder blade or it might have taken a major piece of it.

"Well fuck me! You're a fucking war hero. Let me go get you that pint my son!"

As the old fella left, Fin cast a wistful gaze at the back of the red-haired piano singer as she finished up her tune and headed back to the kitchen. He didn't think she'd seen him, but he couldn't be too sure.

Old Iain arrived back with a fresh new pint and something else, something that drew Fin's eye sharply—a dram of Scotch whisky. Iain plopped into the booth setting the glass down on the table between them, cracking some joke about making the world safe for oil companies. Fin couldn't take his eye off the golden nectar in front of him, willing himself not to reach for it. He knew better.

He could sit and have a few pints, no worries, but whisky had become a problem. The last time he'd touched it he'd not known when to stop. Birt had taken care of him, in a fashion, but he knew he had no control when it came to whisky.

He glanced at the door to the kitchen again, remembering why he was here, and reached for his pint instead. The smell of the whisky drew him, called to him and he knew he needed to do something about it before it was too late. He pushed the glass back toward Iain, "Need to stay off the hard stuff mate, doctor's orders. Thanks for the pint though, aye."

"Ah fuck those cranks, that's pure medicine boy, it'll cure what ails ya!"

They were interrupted by a surge of noise from the growing crowd, calling her back out, "OONA! OONA! OONA!"

They wouldn't be happy until she sang for them, so Oona started to head out of the kitchen again into the chaotic main room of the pub, then stopped to whip off her grubby apron and toss it on the counter. As she did she noticed a bit of gravy that had splattered onto her arm and turned back to the sink to wipe it clean. As she hurriedly washed her hands she fretted at the state of her cracked and chewed fingernails. Not much she could do about that, working in a kitchen and worrying all the time. Not much she could do about the gravy stain that contrasted sharply with her light blue t-shirt.

The crowd in the main room of the pub bellowed her name and stamped their feet, drawing a crimson blush to her plump, freckled cheeks. On catching sight of her as she pushed through the swinging door, they whistled and cheered, which only deepened her blush, spreading it down her neck and bringing out blotchy red patches on her upper chest. She knew she was blushing of course, which only made her blush harder.

The crowd settled as she took her place next to her father, who had picked up his fiddle and tucked it under his jaw.

The men in the room—a mix of estate workers, locals from the town and tourists who came to hear her father's singing—drank in her unconventional beauty along with their pints—her deep red hair, the grace of her movement and stance. Many who didn't know her had tried their luck, only to discover her tongue was as sharp as the cooking knives she used in the kitchen. She would never make it as a model, Fin thought, not unkindly, not in a world that sought beauty in cocaine-snorting, chemically tanned hunger strikers. But her full breasts and the fall of her hips had no lack of admirers he noted, surprised by the intense jealousy he felt.

As her father tuned his fiddle, Oona's eyes swept the front room of the Poacher's Pint, taking in people she knew and those she didn't—a few tourists, some regulars and a vast collection of scruffy-looking musicians. Many of them secretly loved her, and nursed wounds from her reproaches. She confused them endlessly, with free and easy laughter at their jokes and stories, matched with bouts of brooding solemnity when she refused to sing, or to talk to anyone. No one missed the fact that these mostly came when Finlay McColl was away.

She nearly missed him.

He always sat so still! Unnaturally still. The eye wanted to skip over him, seeking instead colour and movement, the brain registering his rock-still form as an inanimate object. Nothing so totally motionless and impassive could be alive.

But when she caught his eye, his gaze burned her, despite his seemingly dispassionate face. She felt the deep complex spirit of the man that lurked behind those simple dark eyes. No one knew him like she did and no one ever would because he had never let anyone else in. No one else had ever felt his love, or his pain. Just her.

The flag draped casket containing the bullet-ridden body of Lachland McColl was carried by six soldiers in formal regimental regalia. They stepped forward to the time of a single sombre drumbeat. As they reached the gravesite, they carefully settled the casket in its cradle over the open grave, then stepped back smartly, while a lone piper began to play.

Standing next to his mother, eight-year old Finlay McColl pulled his hand free from hers and snapped a perfect regulation salute along with the casket bearers. His mother, lost control of her emotions and began to weep openly.

Fin looked up at his mother and the first fat tear welled up out of his eye and ran down his cheek. But he did not weep, he held his salute until the honour guard snapped theirs' back into place.

Dougie MacLean, the owner of the local pub and one of his father's closest civilian friends, stepped forward to put his arm consolingly, respectfully, around Elizabeth McColl's sobbing frame.

Fin clenched his jaw and refused to cry.

He felt a hand slip into his and turned to look. Dougie MacLean's daughter Oona stood there, not looking at him. She was crying too. He remembered how much she had cried when she lost her mother. He didn't take his hand away.

The crowd fell silent as Oona's father drew the bow across his fiddle and she opened her mouth to take a deep breath. They had chosen a simple traditional ballad of a man going off to war in support of Prince Charlie, never to return, leaving behind an infant son and a grieving widow. The crowd loved it when she sang old sad ballads this time of night, when the drink had started to take hold and they wanted to feel something.

She sang the Gaelic verse, then the English, swapping back and forth through the song. The haunting fiddle, her sweet husky voice and lamenting lyrics wove into an emotional spear point, piercing the armour of even the most hardened and cynical listener. She felt each word as she sang it, tears running freely down her cheeks, hanging there for a moment before dropping onto her t-shirt.

When the final lament of the widow died away, *"Oh what will I do now, Oh Lord, now I am alone,"* no one moved for several breaths. The assembled crowd sat in melancholy silence. Finally someone began to clap, then cheer, then everyone in the place jumped up whistling and cheering, pounding tables and stomping feet.

Their cheers warmed her, and she favoured them with a radiant smile, transforming her solemn green eyes into merry emeralds. Her smile stayed until her searching eyes found Fin, sitting in a booth in the corner. He hadn't moved an inch since she'd started to sing. His face looked slack and indifferent and his expression totally unfeeling. Oona's heart fell straight into her gut, the smile dropping off her face as if it had never existed.

She hadn't touched him at all. Suddenly he seemed a stranger, just another drinker in the pub, and a dangerous, frightening one at that.

But then, he moved to bring his pint to his lips, his eyes not leaving hers. As he did so, she saw there, on his face, the wet tracks of tears glinting in the pale yellow light of the chandeliers.

The smile took its place on her face again, and she nodded as their eyes met.

He returned the barest of nods without altering his nonchalant expression, and turned away to his companion.

Well practiced in hiding his emotions, nothing gave away how Fin felt inside as Oona slipped into the booth opposite of him. She looked serious, a bit tense even, and she definitely looked like she had something to say. But no one who looked closely could miss the love in her eyes.

"How long you home for then?" she asked, her words clipped and terse. She wanted to punish him for showing up here without warning. She was tired of him doing that, why couldn't he call like a normal boyfriend? And for staying after closing time, presuming he still had a right to her after months of silence. She didn't know if she could keep it up, but for now her confusion and anger at his distance and random appearances dominated.

He paused and sighed. He knew he was in the shit. "Just a few weeks, maybe a month. I'm here with a mate, Birt. He's up at the cottage …we're taking some rest and relaxation." He didn't want to tell her about his injury. But she wasn't fooled, she's already noticed the edge of the bandage near his neck.

"What happened?" she asked, a bit too anxiously, kicking herself for it.

He met her eyes for the first time, raising one eyebrow and giving a little shrug.

She stared back into his dark brooding eyes and slowly nodded. He couldn't tell her of course. She didn't even know what service he was in—she knew it wasn't just Parachute Regiment like he said. She ran through all the other questions she'd asked before that he couldn't answer: When would he be back? How long would he be away? How dangerous was it? What would he be doing?

She imagined that he would get in trouble for telling her anything at all. Well, fuck it. She had a couple of weeks, more days at one time than since he'd joined the army, she had to make it count.

"Dad's happy to see you," she said, changing the subject. "He wants to retire you know, just play his fiddle and teach. He doesn't want to run the Poacher's Pint anymore."

Fin sat back and let the tension pass out of him. He knew everything would be OK now, but he wondered why she'd brought up her dad.

"That's cool. He staying in Dunfeldy?"

"Uh huh … Where would he go? He's not the type to retire to Spain, he just needs someone to manage the pub for him. He doesn't want me to do it since I started back to Uni part time …"

Fin jerked in his seat. She wrote to him all the time, despite the fact that he rarely answered, but she'd never said a word about going back to school. "Stirling?" he asked.

"Yeah, finishing the nursing finally."

All she'd ever wanted to be since they were kids was a nurse. She'd finished her BSc but she'd never gone on to get her nursing qualification. He didn't know what to say, he was quietly thrilled and wanted her to be happy more than anything. He finally gave her one of his rare smiles, "Good on ya, Oona, that's great news."

"Yeah well … Dad still needs someone to run this pub for him."

He finally figured out what this was really about. She wanted him here, to stay and run the pub. He looked around at bare wooden floor, rough hewn tables worn smooth from use, the soft worn leather booths, the tiny bar in the corner, the old upright piano opposite, all the pictures of Highland glens alongside all the boys from this village who'd gone into the services, and sighed.

He was ready to come home. It really was his idea of pure heaven to stay here, cook, pull pints, listen to Oona's father play and sing, maybe do some deerstalking for the estate … pure heaven. He'd do it. Someday.

"Tell you what, I'll talk to him after this deployment, on my next leave."

She flushed, her eyes growing wide, "Really?" she said, flat, ironic, not really asking.

"Really," he answered, not saying that his next home leave might not be for several months, maybe over a year. Unless he got wounded again or something.

She reached across and took his hand, pulling him out of the booth with her as she stood, pulling him towards her, inviting him to put his arms around her.

It would have been plain rude not to oblige her.

Andy Skeen

The loser gets the good news

Scottish Highlands, present day

The next morning saw Fin and estate gamekeeper Stevie waiting outside Fin's mum's cottage. Stevie, who grew up with Fin, working as a ghillie then a gamekeeper, was smoking to stave off the cold.

Fin tried to shake out the cob webs since he'd not slept much, not with Oona so deprived and demanding with him back in her life all of the sudden. He'd just got up and pulled on his standard issue army cold weather gear. They had planned on going out deerstalking with Stevie who was now responsible for managing the estate's burgeoning population of deer and had invited them along for old times' sake.

Stevie wore his usual outfit for culling deer, as opposed to taking out paying guests: army surplus camouflage. A life on the hill kept him thin and wiry, just like Fin. In their youth, with their similar builds and dark features, many around the estate couldn't tell them apart, and indeed they rarely were apart until Fin joined the army and Stevie took his spot on the estate staff.

The wait got to be too much for him, "What's yer friend up tae?"

"Not a clue," he answered.

Stevie held the lead of a fat Highland pony named Shitehead, although he didn't call the pony that in front of the estate's well-to-do paying guests. Stevie's long-standing hatred of the stalking ponies was an equally long-standing joke among the estate staff.

Fin had fished out his old stalking rifle for the day on the hill, a solid American-made .30-06 former service rifle that dated back to the Second World War. Despite all his experience with some of the world's best long-range sniper rifles, he still shot better with this old rifle than anything he'd ever used in the military, something that never ceased to amaze him. But then his father had tuned the rifle up for him.

The low-magnification scope was fine for the hill. They always got close, no long shots for him since it was too easy to wound a deer, which would only suffer and die a slow painful death. Always better to give them the good news up close for a clean fast kill.

The door to the cottage finally opened and Birt popped out, his usual grinning self, like it wasn't 5 o'clock in the morning and he hadn't been on the piss until a few hours before. Somewhere he'd found a complete set of formal shooting clothes, draping himself from head to knee in a fine woollen tweed shooting suit and deerstalker hat, with long woollen socks coming up to meet his plus-fours just below the knee. He'd finished off the outfit with an old-fashioned set of heavy leather hobnailed Highland walking boots.

Stevie and Fin both burst out laughing.

"Mate, where d'ya get that stuff? You look like a right fucking twat!" Fin spluttered through gasping laughter.

Birt just smiled his usual wide smile, picking a small piece of imaginary lint off the beige tweed lapel, "Fuck you. Just because you have no style, no class."

"Mate, you're from a fucking toilet in Glasgow, where did you get your style from then?" Fin shot back, still chuckling.

"I'll have you know, in India, my family are great warriors, tribal elders even."

Stevie broke in, "Well, if your Lordship is finally ready tae go, the deer are nae goin' tae stand around waiting tae get shot."

On the hill, mist clung to the peaks as the massive landscape swallowed the four tiny figures. Three men and one fat pony trailed through the heather as they headed up to the high places in search of the Scottish Red Deer.

Although he'd looked at it throughout his young life, the scale and beauty of the Highland landscape never failed to move Fin. Some referred to the Highlands as a water desert, denuded of trees. The remnants of the ancient forest, preserved in the peat, stuck out here and there, the cold bony roots and stumps appearing sharp and white against the black peaty mud.

He'd gone to the last remnants of the old Caledonian forest at Kinveachy once, just to see what the Highlands looked like before the trees died, or were cut down. He felt like a tree hugging nutter, but walking among those majestic pines he also mourned the loss of the Highland forests. He thought the egotistical English whacko that was trying to reforest his nearby estate as an extension of his own ego, or perhaps to assuage the guilt of his greed and exploitation through his business career, maybe had a good idea. It would certainly be better for the deer.

The Red Deer belongs in forests and the stark empty Highlands contributed to their smaller average size compared to their genetically identical lowland cousins. It was the poor fodder for the deer and lack of natural predators that led the estates to have to cull them in the first place, or they would overgraze the landscape and the entire population would crash into starvation. Thankfully, plenty of rich Brits, Germans and Americans were happy to pay thousands for the privilege of doing something that had to be done anyway, which provided people like Stevie with a job.

Several exhausting, cold, wet and miserable hours later, Stevie sat quietly glassing the hillside with a long old-fashioned extendable pirate-like telescope. Fin and Birt both used military-issue binos.

"Just there," Stevie finally whispered.

This excited Birt no end, his first view of a Red Deer in the wild. He'd grown up just a few hours drive from the Highland estate, but had never seen a wild deer, "I see them!"

Fin hushed him, "We'll have to circle up and come at them downwind."

His announcement resulted in a long crawl through mud and heather to avoid being scented by the always-alert deer. Several times Fin had to grit his teeth, and he wondered perhaps if he wasn't a bit daft to be out deerstalking when his wound still occasionally bled. He had bumped it on a rock and several bits of heather and what had been a quiet ache now became a dull thudding pain.

Birt wasn't too happy either. "Fuck this shite, mate, look at my clothes. I hate the Highlands. I thought you said this was the sport of Kings." He wasn't grinning anymore.

"Button it Sergeant, or I'll tell Lachie this was your idea."

They eased their way up to the crest of a small ridge. They could hear the deer bellowing around the glen, with challenges and answers among the big rutting stags.

Fin eased his rifle forward, and peered through his scope. A massive unseen stag bellowed a challenge, so close that Birt jumped. The stag held his head low, shaking his massive rack of antlers, keeping watch over a harem of fifteen to twenty female hinds.

Stevie put his hand on Fin's shoulder and whispered softly, "There's another stag just there at the top of the burn, coming towards the dominant stag. Got him?"

Fin nodded.

"Let's wait and see what happens."

The approaching challenger bellowed his defiance and stomped towards the dominant stag. The two turned and marched in unison, shoulder to shoulder, eyeing up each other's size and condition. Neither stag stood down and the dominant stag rushed the challenger, his massive antlers aimed solidly at his exposed flank.

But the challenger was young and quick and turned on his heels to meet the charge squarely and the two majestic stags joined battle with a crash that echoed through the glen.

Despite his youth and vigour, the challenger recognised his error quickly when he felt the power of the monarch of the glen. He turned tail and scooted up the hill directly towards the waiting guns.

The imperial stag pursued for a few perfunctory metres, then turned and pranced victorious and arrogant towards his waiting ladies.

Stevie nudged Fin, "He's all yours Fin, give the loser the good news. He's a rubbish stag anyway, he'll never mate."

But Fin hesitates for a moment, "You take him Birt," he whispered.

"You sure mate?"

"Aye, and hurry the fuck up."

Birt didn't need a second confirmation, and he settled into his rifle, the borrowed estate rifle, a hard-kicking .270. He calmed his breathing, and laid the cross hairs right on the losing stag's engine room, just behind the shoulder where the heart pounded away.

The stag looked away, staring down forlornly at all the female deer being chased about by the massive stag that had defeated him.

He didn't even feel the 140 grain soft point bullet that ripped through his chest and exited the other side to find a home in the heather just beyond. He fell where he stood, the complete loss of blood pressure causing him to pass out immediately and pass on only seconds later.

Birt allowed himself a moment of solemnity at the killing of the deer, but also satisfaction that it had been a clean humane kill. One shot, one kill. And not a bit of the carcass would be wasted. Stevie had introduced him to the boys at the larder who would process the carcass into meat to sell in the estate shop. The hide would go off to be tanned and used for leather and the antlers would be sold to tourists, or made into knife handles. Even the scrotum, penis and testicles would be used as they were highly prized in Chinese medicine. The burgeoning deer population of the Highlands would continue to fuel its economy, just as it had for centuries.

As Stevie cut the penis and testicles free he gave the traditional deerstalker joke for Birt's benefit, "you'll not be needing them nae more."

With the deer 'gralloched,' the Scots word for removing the innards, and the carcass strapped to the pack pony, a process accompanied by much worse cursing than any sailor could come out with, the trio headed down off the misty hillside.

"Why didn't you take the shot pal?" Birt finally asked.

Stevie also chipped in, curious as this wasn't the cool deerstalker that he'd grown up with. "Aye Fin, we took the loser, the weaker one, the cull stag, that's the best thing for the herd."

"Yeah, I know Stevie, I guess I thought Birt should have a go." But truth was, he'd just not had the heart. Maybe he was getting old or going soft, but the stag had been sub-standard and probably would never have gotten laid. The poor fella had just had his arse kicked by a bigger bully and Fin just didn't have the heart to pull the trigger on him. 'Yep, I'm going soft,' he thought.

Birt sensed weakness, a chance to needle his sergeant a bit. "You goin' soft mate? Ya fuck up your heid too?"

Fin turned at him with a rueful but not unfriendly grin, "Why don't you take your best shot pal, we'll see."

Oona jerked awake.

She'd heard a strange sound—rhythmic dry grinding. Rain lashed against the windows. Turning her head from side to side, she couldn't identify the strange sound or where it was coming from. It seemed muffled and to come from inside her head. Childish fear started to build inside her until she rolled over to grasp Fin and realised it was coming from him. Specifically, it was coming from his mouth. He was grinding his teeth.

As she slipped her arm across his chest she realised he was soaking wet. At the contact he snapped upright in bed and let out a shout of rage and sorrow. In his violent move his shoulder caught her face, knocking her sideways and nearly off the bed.

He continued to shout and eventually words formed, He was shouting "no" over and over.

She was seeing stars from the blow to her face, but she felt driven to comfort him, hold him. She wrapped her arms around him, holding him tightly and began to sing quietly and gently, the Ballad of Colloden in Gaelic.

His shouts slowly turned to sobs, but she just kept singing, rocking back and forth holding him tightly.

"It was him Oona, it was him!"

"Who Fin, who? What's happened?"

He was still shaking as he began to tell the story of that day, so many years ago in Iraq when the man who'd killed his father called down the artillery raid that had killed so many civilians.

"It's never bothered me before, I don't know why it is now, but I was dreaming of that day. Only all the Iraqi militia looked like Trentworth and I shot them all, I killed every last one."

"It's never bothered you before?"

"I thought about it often enough, aye. But I didn't stop long enough to let it get to me. I didn't relax, or I drank."

She didn't know what to say to that so she just stroked his hair and neck. Birt had disappeared off for a few days down to Glasgow to visit family, He'd also mentioned something about more "introductions", which Fin took to mean more eligible young women. Fin had pretty much moved into Oona's flat above the Poacher's Pint. Her father had more or less retired to a cottage, interestingly close to his mother's. Fin had decided not to pry too deeply into that one. If they took some comfort in each other's company who could possibly hold it against them?

*

It was the day of the Referendum. He'd decided to vote for it. He thought it would probably all go to shit, but at least the

Scots wouldn't have anyone to blame. He thought they probably deserved to have a shot at running their own show so what the hell.

Between his mother's cooking, Oona's vigorous nightly ministrations and long walks on the hill culling deer with Stevie and Birt, Fin began to almost feel himself again. He also felt something new, a belonging and a contentment that he could never remember having felt before.

He stopped waking up in the night shouting, with visions of those dead women in Iraq. He stopped seeing the eyes of the young boy, the human shield, he'd shot through to kill a gunman in Afghanistan before the bastard could kill more British boy soldiers. Fin also stopped seeing his father, shaking his head at him, disappointed at his weakness.

Oona was always there, ready to sooth him back to sleep, holding him till he quieted and soon the nightmares disappeared altogether. She cleaned his wound for him and kept an eye on his stitches, taking them out for him when he refused to go back to the doctor.

One afternoon, sitting in the pub watching Oona work and he realised he'd had enough, that he'd done his bit. He was tired of being an 'asset', having his leave cancelled at the last minute, never having any sort of normal life. When he was younger he'd loved it and none of the shit mattered at all. He just wanted to vent his rage on the world. Kill or be killed. And like most of his buddies, he was hooked on the rush of it and couldn't get enough. Even sitting on the bar stool, he kept checking the door, watching people's hands, always alert and he wondered if he'd ever be 'normal', if he would always be that way. But maybe he could, maybe this pub and this woman could be it for him. Maybe he could have a family and a normal life.

"How long you staying then Fin?" Dougie, Oona's father asked.

"I've got six more weeks rest leave Mr. MacLean, then I'll need to be getting back.

Dougie set two Edinburgh Crystal glasses on the side table and eased out the cork of a thirty-year-old bottle of Lagavulin. "Aren't you a bit grown up now to still be calling me Mr. MacLean?"

Fin just smiled, dodging the question. "That stuff is too good for me Mr MacLean.

"Nonsense. This is a special occasion, it deserves the best."

"What occasion is that?"

Dougie smiled, "You asked to see me young Finlay, what would that be about then?"

"I've got a fair bit saved up Mr. MacLean—".

"Son, you better learn to call me Dougie, or Douglas if you prefer or I might get offended."

"Yes sir."

"And you better not call me sir again either."

"Yes … Dougie."

"Go on then."

"Oona mentioned you might be interested in retiring, selling off your interest in the pub."

"I've given Oona half."

"Aye."

"And you would like to buy my half."

"Yes sir." Dougie let that one slide, deep in thought.

"Is that it? Nothing else."

Fin was silent, unable to find the right words.

"You see son, I'd always hoped to sell that to Oona's husband."

"Yes sir, there was something else I wanted tae ask you."

The last few weeks had one positive benefit, Fin thought: water falls.

They drove along through the Great Glen and long white ribbons of frothy Highland water spilled down over the granite against the bright greens and purples of spring heather. The drive to Fort William and the cemetery there took them through the most beautiful part of Scotland for Fin.

Birt had shown up and respectfully asked to join Fin, his mother and Oona on the trip to visit Lachland McColl's grave. He felt an affinity with every Victoria Cross soldier and he wanted to pay his respects too. He held his tongue though and tried to remain inconspicuous and not intrude.

Fin and Oona walked hand in hand in front through the gravestones, while Birt escorted Elisabeth McColl arm in arm.

The gravestone had a chiselled bas-relief of a Victoria Cross under Lachland McColl's name and dates of life and death. June 14, 1984, the date a stark reminder that he had died needlessly on the day that the Argentine Garrison had surrendered, led by a young, headstrong Lieutenant named Trentworth. They all knew the story now, of how Trentworth had overstretched them and led them into an ambush on rocky terrain, and of how Lachie McColl had given up his life to save his fleeing platoon. When they got the body back from the Argentineans, it had over thirty bullet holes and seven bayonet wounds. The after action report following the surrender noted that he had accounted for over twenty enemy soldiers dead or injured before they overran his position.

Liz and Oona had brought flowers, Fin had a flask with small pewter cups. After they cleaned the headstone and removed the old bouquet, replacing it with the new ones, he pulled out the flask and they all shared a drink of the 30-year-old Lagavulin that Dougie had offered for the occasion. Then he solemnly poured out a measure, toasted the grave and poured it into the grass.

Birt thought the whole thing quiet, dignified and respectful. He'd never seen anything quite like it. But he couldn't fail to notice the tears on Fin's face, nor how he seemed to clench his jaw and grind his teeth in silence.

Later, back at the pub and after several toasts to Lachie McColl, to the various regiments of Scotland and to 7 Troop of the SAS, Dougie MacLean stood and asked for packed pub's attention. Every worker on the estate had come, even the owner's son Charles.

"My friends. I have known this man here, Fin McColl, son of Lachie and Liz McColl, for all thirty-five years of his life. I've watched him grow and become the man he is, following his father onto the hill as a deerstalker, then into the army. Now I have the great pleasure, along with his mother Elisabeth, to announce that he has asked for my daughter Oona's hand and she has accepted."

The crowded roared its approval, turning its gaze to the happy couple. Birt couldn't believe what he was hearing and his mouth hung open. For his part, Fin noticed that Dougie's arm had gently found his mother's waist and she had stolen a quick kiss after he'd finished speaking. And he approved of the blush of happiness on her face. She'd been haunted by the loss of her husband for so many years. It looked and felt like a great cloud was lifting. It would take him some time to extricate himself from the Army, but he had nearly twenty years in now since he'd joined when he was sixteen. They would let him go if he wanted to go. The Regiment would bin him when he was 40 anyway.

He turned and looked down at Oona's beaming face and raised his glass to the room.

Office of the First Minister, Edinburgh, present day

The effete and refined French Consul General to Scotland strode briskly into Gregor McAdam's office with a smile and an extended hand.

"First Minister, let me be the first to congratulate you on your success!"

McAdam was made a bit wary by the hastily arranged visit of the Consul General, he wondered what this was all about.

"Thank you Consul, and thank you for coming to see me," switching to French, "Would you like a café?"

"Thank you, that would be very nice. I'd forgotten how good your French is Monsieur McAdam." They had met before at some function or other and Gregor had used his French then, to show the Consul General that not everyone in the UK was rubbish at foreign languages. He buzzed Jean and asked for two double espressos.

"To what do I owe this pleasure Monsieur Gilbert, surely you didn't come down from the Consulate just to congratulate me?"

"Indeed no Monsieur," warming to this polite Scot. Not what he expected at all. "It is a delicate matter you see. We, that is, my … colleagues and I … do not believe you will succeed."

McAdam's heart rate was up now, this was unusual, "What do you mean."

"Hmm, I cannot be explicit. Let us just say that there are powerful forces arrayed against Scotland's independence. More than you realise. However ... my colleagues ... this is not an official position you understand, but my colleagues would look favourably upon your success. You would have support from us ... and from our ... friends ... in Brussels. It's a delicate matter because of our own situation."

McAdam knew Gilbert was talking about Basque separatists in France and Spain. The French couldn't overtly support Scottish independence because to do so would bolster the claims of their own ethnic minority Basques in their push for a homeland.

The Consul continued, "However, this is a particular situation. Scotland is already a nation, joined to the UK by a treaty, which, despite the people of Scotland voting to end that treaty, the UK is steadfastly refusing to negotiate its end. Am I correct thus far?"

"You are correct, but I am hopeful they will come to the table."

"Our analysis leads us to believe there is no way that the UK will easily allow you to leave. I'm here to tell you, informally, that ... my colleagues ... would seek to support you and perhaps recognise Scotland's independence ... should you declare it."

Gregor needed time to think and luckily the espressos arrived at that moment. He took his time, adding a couple of sugars, stirring them in slowly. The French, and indeed the Germans, had vested interests in diminishing the powers of the UK within Europe. British intransigence on a whole variety of issues had for decades thwarted the French-German bloc's plans for increased political and economic unification. So, here they were, offering, in not so many words, to support a unilateral declaration of independence by Scotland, should it come. Indeed, the Consul seemed to imply that he could engineer EU recognition of Scottish independence, although Gregor was a bit unclear on the rules behind that.

But in the face of the Prime Minister's total stonewalling of negotiations since the Referendum, to the point of all but declaring the result null and void, Gregor wasn't left with too many options. The result of the Referendum bound him by law and morality to put the desire of the Scottish people into effect.

"Well, thank you for stopping by Monsieur Gilbert. I think I understand what you are saying. Please inform your ... colleagues, that I will take it under advisement and that the proposed course of action is currently under serious consideration."

The Consul sipped his espresso noisily and smacked his lips. "Wonderful café Monsieur McAdam," he said with a smile, "You and Madame McAdam must come to our house for supper sometime very soon. I will send you an invitation."

"I'm sure we'd enjoy that Monsieur Gilbert, we will look forward to it."

"Well then, I will show myself out."

No. 10 Downing Street, London, present day

"Sir, this has just been hand delivered from GCHQ."

"Thank you June," Prime Minister Gordon said, taking the sealed confidential file from his personal assistant.

He opened and read with great interest and growing alarm about the meeting between the Scottish First Minister and the

French Consul General to Scotland. Those scheming frog bastards! How dare they meddle in internal British affairs!

He was going to have to do something, perhaps something drastic, about this before the situation got out of hand. Foreign countries meddling in domestic affairs called for a robust response.

Rage and vengeance

Scottish Highlands, present day

Fin and Birt walked into the pub for a celebratory pint after a good day on the hill. The pub was packed, but silent, except for the TV. He caught Oona's eye behind the counter, but she ignored him, turning away. She always felt too shy to show public affection. She hated the questions about their future and how it was going between them, even now that they were engaged.

"What's going on?" Fin asked the assembled drinkers.

They hissed in unison, "Shhhhhhhhh!"

On the television the Prime Minister was holding a press conference.

" . . . unilateral action taken by the Scottish Parliament would be both illegal and immoral. If Scotland declares independence without negotiation or consultation, His Majesty's government will be forced to suspend the Scottish Parliament. All powers granted to the Scotland Executive will immediately revert to His Majesty's Government in London."

Many people in the pub could not hold their anger, shouting and pounding on tables. Others tried to shush them to hear the rest of the speech.

" … because of reports of violent extremists arming themselves, as a precautionary measure under the Terrorism Act, I have appointed General Edward Trentworth, recently returned from his command of His Majesty's Forces in Afghanistan, to oversee the security situation in Scotland. He will take command of all Scottish police and security forces."

At that, the massed press corp. could contain themselves no longer and began shouting out questions and the press conference descending into chaos.

Oona had watched Fin carefully during the speech as he began to shake and turn red.

Under his breath, so quietly that no one heard him, he whispered, "No."

Then he slammed his open hand down on the nearest table, upsetting drinks and scaring their owners off their stools.

"No No NO! Not him!"

Fin burst from the front door of the pub, murder in his eyes, Oona right behind him, with Birt following at a distance.

His outburst scared her, she'd never seen him like this before, but she knew the story of that General and Fin's father. "Where are you going Fin? Don't do this Fin, please don't do this. You're still wounded, please, you don't have to do this!"

He turned back and the look on his face stopped her cold in her tracks. But she went on bravely, "Look, you're bleeding through your shirt. Come on back inside Fin, please. Let me clean it up."

He stared at her for a moment, not really seeing her, not really hearing her, then turned to Birt, "Get in the fucking car."

Birt looked back and forth between the two lovers, trying to decide what to do, "Where we goin' mate?"

"Back to Hereford. Get in the car."

Birt jumped in and they peeled away, leaving Oona weeping in the car park. All the other drinkers had followed her out and watched with her in quiet silence until Oona's father came up and put his arms around her from behind. She turned and buried her face in his shirt, sobbing. She thought maybe she'd get to keep him this time, but she'd lost him again, maybe forever.

Birt had been silent for the hours it had taken them to get to the border, waiting for Fin to cool off. By the time they got to the border, the crowd there had grown with more protestors and banners. "What are you going to do?"

"I don't know. I'll leave you at HQ though. You don't need to get mixed up in this shit."

"The fuck you will, it's my country too. Besides, where you go, I go. You wouldn't know how to find your fucking socks without me."

Special Forces HQ, Hereford, England, present day

Fin easily defeated the security of the regiment armoury and small arms cage while Birt kept watch. He felt bad about the headache the armoury officer would have in the morning, but not too bad.

They used penlights to ruffle through the armoury, picking out sub-machine guns, M203s, grenades, plastic explosives and timers. Fin headed to the back and picked another lock to a separate area. He emerged with a massive padded rifle case over his shoulder, carrying two metal ammo boxes marked ".50 cal. FMJBT – sniper".

A voice from the darkness stopped him in his tracks.

"Where the fuck you going with that then?"

A stocky grizzled figure moved towards him. Fin could just make out an outline, holding a pistol.

Fin recognised him, "Lachie."

"Aye, Lachie. Answer the fuckin' question boy. You a vigilante now? A revolutionary? Fancy yourself the next fucking William Wallace?"

Fin didn't have an answer. Lachie carried on.

"You going to throw everything away on some sort of revenge mission to kill Trentworth?"

"It was him you know, in the Falklands. It was him that got my Dad killed."

Lachie lowered the barrel of the 9mm, "Aye, I know pal. I know every fuckin' thing about you. That's why I'm going to let you go, you're not going to kill anyone. Hell, I might go with you."

Fin and Birt shared a surprised look.

"What the fuck did you expect, that I would stay in an English army?"

He walked up and grabbed Fin by the front of his shirt and jerked him forward, causing him to wince at the pain in his wound.

"But you listen to me and you listen good pal. If you hurt one woman, one child or any civilian, I will hunt you down and fucking top you myself. That includes enlisted soldiers in the British Army too. Don't be a fucking idiot, right Pal? If you kill anyone, this whole thing is over and we won't have our independence, we'll just have a civil war and you and I will end up as hunger strikers in an iron cage somewhere.

"Now I suggest you go find Jimmy. That little fuck's going to start a war or get himself killed. He's talking about forming a Scottish Republican Army or some daft shite like that. He needs reining in and he respects you. Off you go, and you remember what I said. I'll cover for you here as long as I can."

Fin and Birt headed to the single men's barracks to look for Jimmy, parking out front. They found him in his room, packing.

Fin spoke first, "Alright Jimmy?"

"Aye, pal, golden. You come tae stop me?"

"Nah mate, we're goin' too."

Jimmy checked the chamber of an automatic pistol, then holstered it and tucked it away inside his smock. "You speak to Lachie? He's going all warm and squishy on us."

Fin grinned, seeming to agree without committing himself, "Here's the thing Jimmy, we can't go killing civilians, or police, or squaddies. Got it."

Jimmy scowled, "You sound like Lachie. They fuckin' started this shite Fin, now someone's got to show 'em what that really means. There's got tae be consequences Fin, there's got tae be." He paused and turned to Birt, not unfriendly now, just curious, "Kinda surprising to see you here Birt."

Birt hadn't lost his wide smile, "It's my country too ya Weegie fuck. But Lachie's right, if we start killing, they'll start killing. Scotland will never be free. It'll be just like Belfast mate. Ten years from now we'll all be in prison on hunger strikes and there'll English troops patrolling my mum's street."

Jimmy shook his head, feeling powerless against the logic of two men he respected, but resentful of it. "Well what the fuck are we supposed to do then, eh?"

Fin smiled, relieved, he had him, "I have an idea or two Jimmy, you're going to have to trust me, right? We're going to do everything we can to stop this shite. But we're not killin' anyone. Except maybe Trentworth."

Jimmy smiled a grim smile at that, "All right Fin, we'll do it your way. I know some people who might be able to help us either way."

"Where we goin' by the way?" Birt asked as they drove out of Hereford.

Jimmy answered, "I know a place, a mate in Edinburgh, rich guy in the Independence Party. He's got a place we can use, an old shooting lodge in the Pentland Hills south of Edinburgh. It's perfect."

Fin glanced at Jimmy in his rear-view mirror, "How well you know him?"

"All my life mate. He's sound."

Just then, Jimmy's mobile rang, playing Scotland the Brave.

"Aye pal? ... Uh huh ... Got it ... Sound."

He clicked off the connection, tucking the phone away, "Mate says they're doing checks at the border, we have to get off the motorway, now!"

Fin took the next exit and headed east for the Northumbria forests that sprawl across the English side of the eastern border with Scotland.

They used backcountry forestry roads in the commercial forestry around the northeast of England to avoid a checkpoint. Fin thanked his lucky stars that his Defender looked exactly like the ones used by the Forestry Commission, as he was sure that they'd been spotted more than once but left alone. The police patrols didn't appear to be taking their job too seriously.

They didn't see any other patrols or checkpoints as they approached Edinburgh, and made it to Jimmy's mate's shooting lodge without incident.

"Says we can use it as long as we need it. I know where the key's hidden."

The Pentland Hills, outside Edinburgh, Scotland, present day

Unpacked and with some hot coffee in him, Fin started to feel better about things. The cold rage that had gripped him had begun to subside a bit, but not completely. He wanted to kill Trentworth so bad he could taste it and his jaw hurt from clenching it. He had begun to imagine his fingers around the fucking cunt's throat.

Jimmy sat reading the paper at the dining table. "The vote's next week boys, the Scottish Parliament is going to vote to overturn the Treaty of Union, with or without London." Jimmy shook the paper, turning the page. Fin noticed Jimmy's hand was shaking a bit and thought he saw a tear in the man's eye. He wondered if it was a tear of pride. Scotland, finally taking action, finally deciding to throw off the yoke as one and regain its dignity.

"This one says the Prime Minister will close down the Parliament if it tries to break away on its own, maybe arrest the Ministers."

Fin looked at the ceiling, "Hmmm. If the Scottish Parliament holds a vote on independence, Trentworth will use police from down south … or send in troops. That's what's coming, sure as shit, they're going to bring in troops."

Birt took a sip of his coffee, "You're running this operation Fin, what are we going to do?"

"We're going to town, we've got some shopping to do. Saddle up. No phones till we can get some pre-paid ones."

"Fine, but we need to stop somewhere, need to meet up with the chap that owns this place. He'll probably have everything you need."

Fin stopped and turned, "Where?"

"His place, in Edinburgh."

"Is that wise? Will he be watched?"

"It's fine, he keeps a very low profile. He gives to the SIP, but he's not done anything other than that. No obvious affiliations with any troublemakers. He's got a self-storage business down in Leith."

Leith, port district of Edinburgh, present day

They drove through Edinburgh's port district of Leith, an area being ruthlessly gutted and converted into a heartless commercial shopping district, filled with shitty cheap modern flats, and approached a security guard manning the gatehouse of a self-storage facility. He stared suspiciously at the Defender as it eased up to his window, "Can I help you gents?" He looked vaguely familiar to Fin and Birt.

Jimmy spoke, "We're here to see Tam, he's expecting us."

"He didnae say nought to me."

"Maybe not, we didn't know when we would get in. Just ring him. I know he's here. Tell him Jimmy's here with the friends I told him about."

The guard stepped back into the gatehouse, pushing the window shut as he picked up the phone. A few seconds later the windows swung open and the guard's demeanour had changed completely.

"Go right in gents, park over near that wall, Tam will meet you at the door."

'Tam' turned out to be big swarthy Tamas Macaulay, who owned the shooting lodge in the Pentlands where they were staying, which he kept for shooting pheasants only. He also owned a successful self-storage business.

But he wasn't alone. In a large unused storage area about fifteen men had gathered. Some were sitting, some standing, some smoking, but all were staring suspiciously at the three newcomers. Some nodded at Jimmy, many looked askance at Birt. Most of the bunch were obviously soldiers, some still in uniform. But a few looked a bit wild eyed and angry.

"Welcome to our little meeting boys."

'What the hell have I got myself into now', Fin thought.

Guns, grenades, a few mortars and explosives were stacked carefully against the walls. He recognised some crates of Czech-made plastic explosive that had found its way into the hands of dissident Irish Republican groups from his several tours in the province.

A soldier still in his Royal Regiment of Scotland uniform, with a Black Watch cap, was field stripping an SA80, revelling in the attention that he was getting from a couple of the younger civilians who looked like they'd never seen a gun up close before.

With growing alarm, Fin realised he recognised two of the faces, and not for the right reasons. They were stalwart and violent dissident Irish Republicans. Three years earlier, he'd spent several months working with the Police Service Northern Ireland (PSNI) trying to track them down. Fergal Cahill and Billy Moloney. Total bastards. They specialised in firebombing businesses and sniping at British soldiers near their Barracks. Fin always marvelled at how little the British public now paid attention to the daily fizz of violence that still typified Northern Ireland. These two had a hand in a lot of it.

"Uh, Tam," he whispered, "What are those guys doing here?"

Tam followed his eye to a group of four men in jeans and dark sweatshirts who were sitting and smoking, glowering back at them. One of them had stripped down an AK47 and was cleaning it.

"Ah, you recognise them I take it?"

"Aye."

"Our cousins from across the water have come over to help us with our little problem."

"I see. You do know what those boys are capable of, eh?"

"Aye, dinnae worry. They've promised to toe the line."

One of them, Cahill, heard the conversation, "Aye, we're on the same side now boyo, what the feck do ya think about that then?"

Fin had been in Ireland many times as a young squaddie and an SF soldier. He'd seen kneecapped boys, women and children dismembered by bombs, and tortured snitches. He'd been shot at, and shot back at men like these many times. Cahill and Moloney made his stomach turn.

"I'm wondering what this has to do with you Cahill?"

"Ah, you know my name then boyo, I take it our paths have crossed before then. Pleasure to meet you properly, like. It has everything to do with us. We have a common enemy now."

"I want to know why you're here."

"I'm here to help you send the English home boyo, what the feck are you doing here if not that?"

Tam stepped forward, everyone in the room was on their feet now, "These men are here at my invitation Sergeant McColl, as are you. Gentlemen, the Sergeant comes to us fresh from His Majesty's Special Forces. Do you think you can agree to set aside your previous hatred of each other for a common cause?"

The obvious leader of the terrorists shrugged, "Means nothing to us Tam. Like I said, we're all on the same side now."

Fin ignored him, couldn't even look at him. "Tam, I just want to know what they're doing here, what you're planning. If we start killing you know where this will go right? I've seen it first hand and we don't want Scotland to go there. We don't."

Another voice cut in, the boy soldier from the Black Watch who knew Fin's name, "We have to fight Staff Sergeant, we have to do something. They're sending in English troops, I know! I heard before I bailed out. They're coming!"

"I know boy, and we need to give them a reason to go home. But if we start killing then Scotland will never be free of it. You ever been across the water Private?"

"Aye, Staff."

"What's your name?"

"Liam Staff, Liam McLaughlin."

"Well Liam, do you want APCs and foot patrols harassing your mum? Do you want Glasgow and Edinburgh to be like Belfast? Or Ulster?"

"No Staff."

Tam cut in, "No one wants that, but if you're not here to fight McColl, what the fuck are you doing here?"

"I didn't say I wasn't going to fight, I just said we shouldn't be killing."

Then it was Birt's turn, "We've both spent the last two years in the Counter Revolutionary Wing. It does some nasty shite when the situation calls for it, but the first thing we learned is that fear of death and violence is a lot more powerful than the reality of it."

"That's it exactly," Fin agreed. "We just need to convince them that staying is not worth it, but without giving them an excuse to pile in heavy, with a full crackdown. They will say that they need to establish security and ensure an orderly transition, all that shite, but what they'll really do is settle in and never leave. I know, trust me."

Tam was ready to believe him, wanted to believe him. He didn't want to kill, didn't want Scotland to go up in flames. "What do we do."

"Right, here's my plan."

When he'd outlined his ideas, directly from the CRW playbook, but with some creative twists he'd learned from the Taliban, he thought he'd won them over. Most of them were grinning.

Not Jimmy though, and not the dissident Republican boys among whom he now stood.

"Jimmy, you with me?"

"For now Fin, for now. This might work. But if it doesn't … we do this my way. We go after them."

Suddenly the Black Watch soldier raised his fist and started shouting, everyone joining in, for they all knew the words.

124

". . . for, as long as a hundred of us remain alive, never will we on any conditions be subjected to the lordship of the English. It is in truth not for glory, nor riches, nor honours that we are fighting, but for freedom alone, which no honest man gives up but with life itself!"

Andy Skeen

Sniper on the roof

Edinburgh, Scotland, present day.

Armoured personnel carriers and troops began off-loading from massive military transports that had landed at Edinburgh airport. Trentworth, in a civilian suit now, watched impassively with the senior military commander, Colonel Tim Robinson.

"Is this really necessary sir?" Robinson asked.

"Don't go soft on me now, we need a show of force. Intelligence suggests that radical nationalist elements are arming themselves. We have to be ready for anything."

Helicopters screamed over the massive crowds that had built up in Princes Street Gardens in the heart of Edinburgh. Searchlights swept over the thousands of demonstrators in the street, and up The Mound into the Old Town of Edinburgh, a medieval stone skyline that loomed over the Gardens against the dark sky.

The original Parliament Building in the Old Town, now part of the Law Courts, had been chosen as the site for the historic vote. The old National Parliament had been the site where the Acts of Union had been passed in 1706 and McAdam and the SIP had decided that that would be where they would rescind them.

On the roof of a Princes Street shop just over a kilometre away, Fin huddled inside a metal blind designed to look like an air conditioner. He even had a fan-unit to make noise like an aircon unit. He eased back the bolt of his sniper rifle, chambering the first round and settled comfortably into the rifle.

As he swept his scope along Princes Street he saw protestors waving the Scottish Saltire and Lion Rampant flags, chanting slogans and screaming in anger at the column of armoured personnel carriers working its way along the street.

From the commanding officer's hardened staff car, Trentworth could see soldiers roping from helicopters, surrounding the National Parliament, just out of view below the skyline in the Old Town.

His radio squawked, "Spearhead is in position, repeat Spearhead is in position. Target perimeter secured."

The chanting deafened him, he couldn't quite hear his radio, but his operations team had it under control. None of the demonstrators looked inclined to approach the heavily armed column as it clanked down Princes Street though. The ground commander for the operation, Colonel Robinson answered, "Roger that, secure the entrances, no one leaves."

"Are you expecting trouble Colonel?" Trentworth asked.

"Not as such sir. But nearly every Scot in the army has deserted, including most of the SF regiments, which are heavily Scottish. And then there are the intelligence reports of radical nationalists sir. It could get a bit interesting if they hooked up sir."

"I see. Satan's minions could pay us a visit eh? We could have an Irish situation on our hands."

"Yes sir. As you know, weapons and explosives have gone missing sir, including some of the new SF sniper rifles."

Trentworth looked out the window at the demonstrators, "Where are the police Colonel, why isn't this crowd under control?"

"There sir," he replied, pointing at the police, standing among the crowd, arms folded, staring back, "Without police security to hold the crowd back, we should withdraw."

"Withdraw? What the hell for? We will fulfil our mission Colonel and damn these traitors to hell," he growled back. He was shaking with rage.

'He's finally lost it,' the Colonel thought to himself, not answering.

As the APCs clanked along, turning up the Mound, Fin spotted the Command Vehicle, festooned with antennae and clicked his scope to a higher magnification. He saw Trentworth's face. Fin curled his lip in anger, his finger moving to the trigger of the big sniper rifle.

Liz and Oona sat together in the lounge of the McColl cottage, Fin's childhood home. The telly showed the scene in Edinburgh, with all the protestors, helicopters and cameras.

The announcer provided a voice over, "The dramatic pictures you're seeing are live from Edinburgh, where the Scottish Parliament has scheduled a vote on whether Scotland should declare independence from the United Kingdom. Lucy Jenkins is on the ground and we have cameras inside where First Minister for Scotland, Gregor McAdam is about to make a speech. Lucy, tell us what you know."

"The crowd here is angry Dermott but excited. Angry about rumours that troops are on their way, but excited to be here, to be close to where this historic vote will take place. We know the voting is about to start, and we know that several military transport aircraft landed at Edinburgh Airport just over an hour ago. One way or another it looks like this crisis is about to come to a head."

The camera cut to inside where the entire Scottish Parliament sat, crammed together in the centuries old tiny building. Many had their arms folded, their faces defiant, as Gregor McAdam began his address. They had heard the news, they knew what was coming, but refused to budge.

"So honourable members, colleagues, friends, it has come to this. Westminster has decided to send in troops and arrest us all . . .

"I say let them come!"

The chamber erupted into raucous and defiant cheering as most of the Members jumped to their feet, although the cameras zoomed in on some members who remained sitting, stoic and glum. McAdam looked defiant as he soaked up the cheers.

"This great and proud nation has toiled under a yoke of colonialism for so long, our national identity suppressed by the weight of the Union with Great Britain."

He waited for silence as many ministers shouted in angry agreement. "Now the people have spoken, both through open elections, and a free and fair referendum. Their voice is clear and it is unified.

"It is the voice of a nation claiming its sovereignty.

"It is a voice demanding its dignity.

"It is a voice, most of all, crying out for freedom!"

The chamber erupted again. McAdam took it in and then held up his hand, asking to continue.

"We, their democratically elected representatives, must move to affect their will. We must now take our rightful place as equals in the family of nations, no longer subservient to a foreign power."

He paused to let his words sink in, his voice going quiet.

"But in their pride, greed and arrogance, our friends to the south will not welcome us into that family.

"They think that our freedom is theirs to grant.

"But, it is not. It is ours by natural right and we shall take it!"

As his voiced boomed through the chamber the members again exploded into cheering, with nearly all of the 129 members standing and clapping, many shaking their fists.

Outside in the gardens and open spaces of central Edinburgh, where hundreds if not thousands of radios and internet-enabled mobile phones and tablets were streaming the television feed, the crowd too roared its approval.

McAdam signalled for the vote to begin, a simple count of raised hands.

"Those in favour of passing The Articles of Independence, rescinding the Act of Union of 1706, please raise you right hand and keep it raised until the counting is complete."

The cameras captured the moment in the packed tiny old Parliament Chamber, well in excess of its fire code maximum attendance, as 120 members of the Scottish Parliament raised their right hand.

The crowd didn't need to wait for the count and thousands of voices joined together to voice their ecstasy. The sound wasn't anything like that of a normal political demonstration. It sounded primal, angry and ecstatic, with animalistic cries and shrieks of an ancient rage unleashed, of ancient invisible chains breaking free, of a 300-year old shame that had cloaked the heart of a nation being put to right.

"120 in favour, 9 abstentions, the Article is declared passed!" McAdam heard the strange lamentations of the crowd and felt it himself. He wanted to join them, and leaned back away from the microphone as it built in his throat, escaping only as a constricted grunt that he swallowed down. When he regained control, he leaned forward into the microphone again, and shouted, "Scotland is free!"

Outside the building, the elated crowd kept well back from the soldiers and APCs that had pushed up to the Mound and had taken it over. The menacing weaponry on show atop the vehicles seemed to have a sobering effect on many, though the whoops of celebration continued.

Trentworth was still twitchy as his staff car came to a stop in the car park on The Mound where they were setting up a temporary command post.

He emerged from the car every inch an aristocratic military officer, looking for his combat commanders. Television cameras from assembled reporters momentarily blinded him and Lucy, the reporter, shoved a microphone at his face, screaming a question he couldn't hear.

He yelled into her face, "Are you insane?! Get back you idiots! Move!"

She flinched away and security officers began to clear a space around the convoy.

"Colonel, deploy your men, make the entry."

Colonel Robinson turned to give his final orders, "Right, we've been through this scenario. These are civilians and we're not expecting trouble, but tell your men to stay alert. Our orders are to occupy the building and arrest the leaders of the SIP, you have the list and photographs. We are to transport them back to the airport for exfil. Move with deliberate haste, get it done and let's get the hell out of here."

Fin was glued to his sniper scope, his finger tightening on the trigger. He kept the well-bred visage of Trentworth, the man who had caused the death of his father, in the scope as the man exited his car, watching as he batted away a microphone and yelled at the many reporters that mobbed him.

In the darkness of his hide, Trentworth's face wavered in his scope. Fin pulled the trigger. The massive report of the big rifle shook his frame, but he'd put in moulded hearing protectors—he'd need his hearing to make his escape.

The rifle's kick jarred his teeth, but he rode the recoil and followed through to bring the scope back on target to confirm a hit. He repeated this action three more times, four shots in just over five seconds.

He dropped the rifle in place and quickly shifted out of his hide. He was scrabbling over the roof to the stairwell when he heard the report of another rifle a few hundred metres away, also on a Princes Street roof, "What the fuck?"

Trentworth turned to Colonel Robinson, about to say something when the empty staff car behind him exploded into flame, throwing him to the ground.

He rolled and looked back, people screaming and running. BOOM! The track of an APC exploded …

BOOM! The engine of an armoured Land Rover exploded further down the column.

BOOM! Another APC track exploded.

Colonel Robinson was there, screaming in his ear, "Keep your head down sir, they've got .50 calibre sniper rifles!!

"I know what the hell he has. There's only one. He's Special Forces, he's not aiming at us. Looks like they have some honour after all."

A lieutenant, the platoon commander, scurried up as Trentworth and Robinson got to their feet, accompanied by a radioman.

"Sir, the shots came from the buildings to the north, there's people everywhere and the police are not responding. There are no major casualties. What are your orders sir?"

Robinson looked to Trentworth.

"He'll be long gone, I suggest you continue the operation, exfiltrate the targets, then get me to the Executive Building and I will try to restore some order to this city. We'll find the bastard later."

The Colonel nodded his agreement, "You heard the man, send in Spearhead to exfil the targets. We'll load up on the undamaged vehicles and get the hell back to the airport."

"Roger that sir!"

At that moment, Colonel Robinson's head exploded in a blast of red mist and gore, his whole body flung backwards against the staff car. Trentworth didn't think twice, he hit the deck and crawled under the staff car in a split second.

The combat commanders didn't react so quickly and two of them were hit with similar results. The heavy inertial energy of the exploding .50 calibre round liquefied their muscle and tissue, tossing their broken frames to the ground like rag dolls.

Fin ducked down, pulling out his mini binoculars, frantically searching the rooftops, trying to figure out who the fuck was firing. He couldn't see anyone so turned his binos back towards the scene below, taking in the dead bodies and mayhem.

Standing in the middle was a Colonel, still alive, issuing orders to everyone around him trying to get the situation back under control. He thought the man cowering beneath a car must be Trentworth.

Fin decided he'd better move off before someone decided to come looking for him.

Emerging from the rear of the building in jeans and a sports top, pushing his mountain bike, he sauntered away like he hadn't a care in the world. That was the key to any disguised evasion, not looking like you were running, not drawing any attention to yourself.

His biggest concern was the blood seeping from his wound, starting to show through his shirt. If anyone noticed it, things could get awkward. It had started to ache as well. If he had to run it might pull open.

He started to think he might get away with it when two Military Police cars screeched to a halt at the end of the street and men jumped from the cabs with SA80 rifles, "Stop where you are, don't move!"

"Get up you idiots, get on your feet! He's long gone!" a platoon sergeant yelled, resisting the urge to kick one of the officers taking cover at his feet. "Get on the radio, let's finish this operation."

His voice of authority got them moving and they quickly entered the old Scottish Parliament building and covered all fire exits, meeting no resistance.

The entry teams were not armed, unlike the heavily armed security cordon. Although they were respectful and restrained, they were firm and businesslike. They had a seating plan and pictures of the SIP cabinet ministers and they arrested them one by one.

For their part the Ministers sat passively, saying nothing, not reacting, simply going limp when they were arrested, handcuffed and dragged away. Television crews captured the entire scene and broadcast it across Scotland and the world.

The entry team commander got on the microphone and ordered the rest of the Ministers to be taken to the busses they had brought up. Most went quietly, some simply went limp and had to be manhandled out of the room.

The Prime Minister watched the scenes of a PR and political disaster unfolding before him. What the hell had he done? Zoë sat beside him, saying nothing. He had been rough with her earlier, taking out his frustration and stress. She'd seemed to revel in it and her attitude towards him had changed since the episode, she was much more demure, meeker. He liked her this way.

"Well? Now what?"

"You can't hold the SIP Ministers, it would be a PR disaster. You could probably keep them under house arrest and limit access to them by citing public safety. Can you use the Terrorism Act? Parliament has passed the Bill to suspend devolution so that's history. Now you should direct the public's anger at the sniper." She jumped up from the couch, "I will start drafting a speech."

"Fine, do it, I'll find out if they have a clue who it was. I better get back. No doubt the Cabinet will want another COBRA meeting."

Houses of Parliament, London, England, present day

The members of the COBRA committee sat looking glum at the Prime Minister.

"Declare martial law."

Stunned silence met the pronouncement by the usually jolly and serene Deputy Prime Minister.

The PM finally spoke, addressing the COBRA committee, "Stephen's right. The police are no longer enforcing the law, they've chosen sides."

COBRA, despite its menacing sounding acronym, simply stood for Cabinet Office Briefing Room A, which was the secure facility in the Cabinet Office buildings on Whitehall. It had sophisticated audio and video links to secure locations or facilities nationwide that could also be used to stream security or intelligence information for the consideration of the Committee. Its members included all the key ministers, plus senior security and intelligence civil servants.

"But William, this is already getting out of hand, won't sending more troops just make it worse? Inflame the situation more?" The PM always thought the Defence Secretary was a bit soft for the job. The man had been in the military for twenty-five years, what the hell was his problem? He also bristled at the man's annoying habit of using his first name, even in formal situations like this.

"We have to establish law and order Jeremy, nothing else can proceed until we do that. I'll have plans drawn up tonight for declaring martial law for your consideration. We will reconvene first thing in the morning to vote on them. It should go without saying that we have to move quickly. Everyone should stay here tonight and be available for decisions that affect your particular ministries as plans are drawn up."

He was confident of getting the votes. There might be a few dissenters, but only a few. He had his cabinet well under control.

Two wheels are better than four

Edinburgh, Scotland, present day

"Stop where you are, don't move!"

Fin turned, maintaining his nonchalant pose, "Sorry?"

"I said stop where you are, put your hands up!"

"Putting on his best 'Trainspotting' accent, "Wah? I'm no doin' nu'in mate!"

"Stop moving, put your hands up now or we will open fire!"

Fin had edged closer to an open alleyway off St Andrew's Square. He then broke and sprinted toward the alley and to their credit the police didn't open fire. He jumped onto his mountain bike and raced down the alley. It led to a small walkway by a pub called the Café Royale. A drunk staggered into the street and he had to smash into him, taking the impact on his shoulder. He burst out onto the east end of Princes Street and sprinted away from the chaos and destruction of Princes Street Gardens to the west.

He had set his bike up carefully for just such a possibility. It was his street bike, built for jumps and tricks on tarmac rather than dirt. With full suspension and hydraulic disc brakes, it gave

him the best possibility of escape in a crowded city like
Edinburgh, with its many stairways and narrow alleys.

A siren picked up behind him as he sped along Waterloo
Place away from Princes Street and the sweeping lights of police
cars told him they had found the scent. He sprinted past the
looming art deco edifice of the old Scottish Office building, St
Andrew's House, where English governors had administered
Scotland since after the war.

Just beyond it lay a staircase and a long steep walkway that
would drop him off Calton Hill and onto Calton Road a hundred
feet below him. As the sirens and lights came up to him from
behind, he made the hard right turn just missing a car coming
towards him from the other direction.

He hopped the curb and braked hard, making the turn onto
the walkway and down the first staircase, nearly shooting off a
cliff into the brush. Two men holding hands jumped out of his
way as he sped down the steep tarmac walkway and he had to
brake hard. The hydraulic disc brakes squealed again as he set up
for the sharp right turn, then left onto Calton Road.

Too late he realised that maybe this wasn't such a great plan
since it had put him right next to the new Parliament Building
and police were everywhere. Luckily they hadn't got the message
yet and he shot past them and into Holyrood Park. The police just
stared. His plan was to head south, get out of town and try to
make it out to the shooting lodge without being spotted. But just
as he neared the top of the hill at the east exit of the park, two
police cars drove onto the roundabout blocking it off. He could
have easily gone round them, but that would leave him exposed
to an easy chase.

Making a sharp left he rode up onto the grass then over a
rocky jump into the gravelled and rocky path that cut through

Arthur's Seat, the remnants of the massive extinct volcano that dominated this part of the Edinburgh skyline. The steep slope and rocky outcrops would stop any motorised pursuit and no one on foot would ever catch him.

The rocky path led downhill all the way to the ring road and spit him out the northeast entrance of the park. He saw more lights in the distance, back by the new Parliament, but no one had made it down here yet. From here it was downhill all the way to Leith. He pumped past the old Velodrome, the bicycle-racing track, where he'd once tried to race. But those guys were pure mental, racing at full speed without brakes. If only they could see him now.

He took a side street that he knew led him all the way down to Leith Links, where, apparently, the rules of golf were really invented, as opposed to St. Andrew's up in Fife.

Only silence greeted him as he rode through this colourful area of Edinburgh. He thought everyone must be up in the town centre, or watching what was happening on the telly. All the better for him. He had a new plan.

The Water of Leith was the name of a small river that ran practically from the shooting lodge in the Pentland hills all the way to Leith, Edinburgh's port district, right through the centre of the city. More importantly, it had a green zone alongside it with a path that was bikable. He'd jogged it many times when he lived in Edinburgh, lots of soldiers did to keep in shape. Most of the roads went over it, with only a few to cross before he made it all the way out of the city. The trees would shelter him from view and any eyes in the sky would have a hard time picking him out. Even thermal imaging would have a tough time since plenty of people walked and cycled along the path.

He'd noticed when they were doing their recon that the path didn't appear on the online maps. It would probably appear on Ordnance Survey maps of course, but he was trusting that no one would think of it, or that the English simply would not know about it.

He sped through Leith and turned onto the path off Tollboth Wynd just as it crossed the Water of Leith. He entered a world that seemed remote from the bustling city he'd left behind. Hard to believe he was still in urban Edinburgh. The river gurgled along beside him and he startled a fox that had been sniffing around near a rubbish bin.

He moved steadily along the Water without incident, about fifteen minutes, until he came to Corstorphine Road. The Water went under, but the path went up onto one of Edinburgh's busiest roads—a major artery that led from the airport to the west right into the city centre. It was crawling with police and ambulances. As he watched from the shadows, an armoured personnel carrier clanked eastward down the road. He was stuck.

Only one place to go now, back to Tam's, back to Leith. He felt wetness on his shoulder and chest and knew that he'd torn open his wounds again. He needed to stop the bleeding and get himself patched up. Hopefully Tam could help.

No. 10 Downing Street, London, England, present day

As the Prime Minister walked to the podium the massed international press corp. unleashed a flash bulb assault that stopped him in his tracks. He covered his need to recover from the maelstrom by seeming to pause for photographers.

He then strode to the podium and held up a hand in gentle supplication for order. He tried to give off a calm but serious presence in the face of crisis.

"I'm here today to announce a series of measures to deal with the crisis in Scotland sparked by a barbaric act of terror in Edinburgh last night. As you all no doubt know, devolution of certain Parliamentary powers to Scotland has been suspended. The mechanism and timing of any return to devolution will be determined by events and a process of negotiation and clarification with the relevant parties in Scotland.

"The Scottish referendum and unilateral declaration of independence have been deemed to be invalid by the Cabinet. In an effort to exercise the will of the Parliament I have directed His Majesty's armed forces, in cooperation with local police, to dissolve the Scottish Parliament and place its former ministers under house arrest, where they will remain for the duration of the crisis.

"During the operation, as you all will have seen from the television coverage, a number of members of the armed forces were killed by a terrorist or terrorists. We are pursuing a number of leads in pursuit of the perpetrators of this act. For the moment we believe that they may be deserters or former members of the armed forces.

"The seriousness of the evident threat demands that we take further measures to ensure public safety and track down these terrorists. To this end I am extending the emergency powers provided to Interim Governor Edward Trentworth, giving him direct command of all military units in Scotland. All matters relating to security and policing in Scotland will now come under his direct control, reporting to Parliament through me.

"I have also promised him full access to the resources and capabilities of His Majesty's police, armed forces and intelligence services in an effort to affect a swift end to this crisis and restore public order.

"Operations are ongoing and I am not in a position to answer questions or provide details that would undermine the effectiveness of these operations. Please rest assured that at the earliest opportunity His Majesty's government will provide full details both to Parliament and the public.

"I will not take questions at this time. Thank you." With that he simply walked away, leaving behind a chorus of shouted questions.

Leith, Edinburgh, Scotland, present day

Fin rolled to a stop in a side alley near Tam's self-storage facility.

Everything hurt, especially his shoulder, but he needed to find out what the hell had happened and who had been shooting. He had an idea.

He had cased the CCTV and observation points around the facility before and knew where he could observe the facility without being spotted. He pulled out his mini binos and took a quick look.

Nothing obvious, no external guards, but he know someone would be watching. They should be expecting him, but if one of them had been the shooter, the reception might not be a warm one. He couldn't see any vehicles except the firm's removals vans.

He decided to chance it and just walk up and knock on the door.

He heard movement inside then the door eased open.

"You alone?"

"Aye"

"Jimmy with you?"

"Nah."

"You seen 'im?"

"Nah."

The door opened further and Tam gestured for him to come in.

"What's gone on here?" Fin asked. "Where's Birt?"

"Jimmy just up and left right after you, despite what we'd agreed. All the hard cases went with him, including the Irish boys. His car was loaded up. We've heard nothing from him. Birt and those that refused to go with Jimmy are up at the lodge waiting to hear from you. I told them to stay up there out of sight for now. What the fuck happened?"

"I shot up the convoy, then it must have been Jimmy that opened up on those officers."

"There'll be those that applaud it, but there could be real trouble now," Tam said, "for the moment, the SLA is with you, but I don't know for how long. Jimmy will have his supporters."

"Aye. We'll need a plan."

"Well, let's go to the office and have cuppa, or maybe something stronger. You look like you need it."

"Aye, and a good first aid kit if you have one."

Andy Skeen

Sharp dressed man

Edinburgh, Scotland, present day

Fin knew Edinburgh. He knew it well, every dodgy pub, every tourist haunt, every place a person could get lost in a haze of whisky—and maybe a lovely student with more money than sense, and a sex drive to match the power of her daddy's wallet.

He'd been stationed here shortly after qualifying as a soldier, aged 17. He'd drunk and fucked his way through the swathes of pubs and women and he'd loved them all. And he missed them all. It had been a revelation, and an education, to discover that girls found him attractive. He'd always thought of himself as a skinny runt, but the girls, especially English and European girls, were drawn to his smouldering eyes and his intensity.

Fin had been in some of the shittiest most deprived places on the planet. But he'd also been in some of the most beautiful and exclusive places in the world on close protection detail of high value assets. He'd come to realise how an outsider could see much of Scotland as a small ugly country—at least when viewed from the choked streets of many of her largest Central Belt cities and towns, away from the historical town centres and before you get to the magnificent countryside.

Monolithic brooding concrete government housing estates—dens of drugs, despair and violence competed with bland pebble-dashed rows of shabby houses to suck the life and happiness out of any visitor to many a Central Belt city.

But Edinburgh, he thought, seemed to buck that trend, at least on first viewing. It inspired many a tourist with its mix of Mediaeval and Georgian magnificence. But as one encounters the layers of parochial provincialism and insular snobbery lurking behind those sailing balustrades and sturdy monolithic edifices, it suffocates creativity and aborts any nascent ambition. Fin had spent several years in Edinburgh as a young soldier and reflected that in all those years he never made a native Edinburgher friend. All his friends were like him, transplants. Edinburghers kept to themselves and ran in tribes based on which school they attended.

Now he had a chance to put his knowledge of the city to use, to disappear, right under the noses of the police and security services. He sported a stubbly beard, skate clothing and his jump bike, with street tyres, with a bandana and sunglasses to round out his disguise. All he needed to perfect the role was act it out. He adopted the smug, vacuous open-mouthed grin of the typical uni student. Despite being over 30, no one in the university district of Edinburgh gave him a second glance.

He cruised the streets with impunity, dodging checkpoints and security details with a combination of his skills as a soldier and his misspent youth of mountain biking and poaching deer in the Highlands.

He stopped at a newsagent to get some papers to find out what was happening and cringed from the front pages. A youthful version of his own face, his first service photo aged 17, stared back at him under his regimental cap. The SAS policy of never letting your face be photographed had saved him. No one would connect that clean-cut smiling uniformed boy with a scruffy skate punk in shades, bandana and a week-old beard.

Birt, on the other hand, looked exactly like Birt, except for a traditional Sikh turban instead of the black bandana he wore on operations. His unmistakably happy smile jumped off the page. Fin hoped that the average Brit thought all Indians looked alike. Ironic that racism might save Birt from detection.

He needed to get out of sight, after getting some more up-to-date information.

The Royal Estate of Balmoral, Scottish Highlands, present day

"What do you think of this Scotty?"

No matter how many times it happened, the fact that the young King asked his opinion on things never ceased to startle the old gamekeeper. He decided to stall for time.

"Think of what Your Highness?"

"I wish you wouldn't call me that Scotty. I thought we'd agreed that you would call me Eddie on the hill, like you used to. And you know exactly what I'm talking about."

Scott McDeigh, fourth generation Head Gamekeeper at Balmoral Castle, kept his eye glued to the long antique brass spotting scope that rested on his tweed-encased knee as he examined every nook and cranny of the Glen beneath him looking for stags. Stalking with the King certainly made for an interesting day. He couldn't remember ever having been asked about anything other than deer in his entire long life of guiding denizens of the Castle out onto the heather-clad hill. Tricky business this opinion asking by Royals.

"Well, I think all those hinds over on Calstoun have pulled the stags out of the Glen and off our patch entirely. I don't see hide nor hair Your Royal Highness Eddie Sir."

"If I didn't know you better Scotty, I would think you're trying to change the subject. I won't judge you and I don't question your loyalty, I really want to know what you think," the young king asked again.

Heaving up his well-earned girth, which daily tested the strength of his Balmoral Tweeds, he closed the telescope and slipped it back into its leather carrying case.

McDeigh considered. What should he say? He thought of his position. He was ready to retire and had no son to take his place. He had squirreled away most of his monthly pay over the years and he and his wife were headed to Spain and the warm summer sun. He felt emboldened by his coming freedom. He could speak his mind, the King had asked him after all.

"Sir, I believe this is all about money and power. Everything is, isn't it? I accept the Monarchy, I always have. You are my King. But the people of Scotland have voted, the referendum has passed. The right way forward seems clear enough to me."

'Yes,' the young King thought, 'I think so too.'

Edinburgh, Scotland, present day

Dressed in a sharp suit and tie, now sporting a tight little goatee beard and bleached blond highlights in his cropped hair, Fin eased himself back into the soft cushions of the swanky George Street wine-bar-cum-nightclub that was so ostentatious and pretentious he didn't know how anyone could keep a straight face standing in it. He pushed his sunnies up as he sat down.

No one gave him a second look since he looked much like most of the men in the place, suited and booted, with a sort of unconscious arrogance bred of financial success. He kept looking at the door—anyone watching would conclude he was looking for his date.

Instead, a dishevelled, overweight, slightly odorous middle-aged man ambled in, scratched his flabby neck where it spilled over his shirt collar as he moved towards the bar. When the man next caught his eye, Fin straightened his tie and the man nodded.

Collecting his pint, the man came over and joined Fin in the black leather booth.

"Right, so who the fuck are you then?"

"Fin McColl."

The reporter nearly spilled his pint down himself again, but managed to miss Fin with the spray. He recovered quickly.

"Good idea, the shirt and tie, I'd never have recognised you."

Fin just nodded.

"Everyone is looking for you, the polis, the army, everyone. I should turn you in right now."

Fin nodded again. "Yes, you should, it's what I would do in your place. But take note that you can't see my hands or what they are holding, and I'm not alone pal. Let's move on from that, eh?"

The reporter's slightly podgy face turned ashen as he remembered the dead men on Princes Street and just exactly what kind of man he was dealing with. But his voice was steady, he was off the hook. He had an excuse not to turn the man in and he could now pursue the story, "So, what do you want to tell me?"

"It wasn't me that did the killing, it was someone else from my Regiment, someone a bit out of control. I shot up the vehicles, that was our agreed plan, but this guy has gone rogue on me."

"Can you prove that?"

"No."

"You got a name?"

Fin looked pained. "I can't really grass a mate … ex-mate. Just go digging, you'll figure it out. It wasn't me, I don't want to hurt anyone. But tell them. Tell the English public, if this continues, more people are going to die. Tell them to let it go, to let Scotland go. I will try to keep a lid on things, keep things from getting too fucked up, but they have to make some moves or this thing will explode. These people are ready to fight and kill, it's stupid to continue to provoke them. There are also Irish Republicans involved. This shit is serious now."

"I can't see it. The PM is set on his path, he can't back down now. Besides, if he does, he's out of power, eh? Nae chance he'll go down without a fight."

"You just write your article. These fuckers are dyin' to start killing," Fin said with a wry smile, "tell the public that, tell them it needs to stop."

The reporter looked non-committal. "I'll report what you've said."

"Then that's enough. Stay in that chair and finish your pint before you get up. Don't touch your phone, I'm not alone, you're being watched."

Fin was bluffing of course, but he also didn't think the guy would call the polis too quickly. The reporter would want to write his story, not watch his story get caught.

One's creative side

Leith, Edinburgh, Scotland, present day

"I delivered the message, for what it's worth. The newspaper hack seems to think it's pointless, that London's not gonna back down." Fin said this to Tam, sitting across from him, but with his eyes firmly locked on the picture of Trentworth on the front page of the paper he was reading. He could smell that Tam had had a dram recently and it awoke a yearning need, which he ignored.

"He's right you know. Maybe we should give them something to think about."

"Aye. I think we need to lighten the tone a bit." Fin knew that mockery would deflate his enemies faster than threats and violence. Many a time in the CRW they had undertaken operations designed to discredit and humiliate an enemy.

"We need to make this whole thing look foolish instead of dangerous. If they fear us too much they'll overreact. We've delivered a threat, now let's deliver a laugh or two. At the same time we can show them what we're made of, remind them who we are in case they've forgotten. Then I want to really hit them where it hurts, cost them some big time money."

"I like the sound of that. Give me some particulars and I'll take it to the Man and see what he thinks."

The Man.

This development had settled Fin's mind considerably. Tam had figured out a way to communicate with the First Minister, despite him being under house arrest. Fin was back in his comfort zone, taking orders from what he considered to be a lawful authority. He didn't want to think about anything else, not his future, not Oona, not anything. He'd shut all that off completely. All he could think about was beating Trentworth, and winning independence for Scotland. It was just another operation in enemy territory, requiring meticulous planning and preparation.

"And by the way, if you need any help, you'll need to take Liam. He's been bugging me since you left to give him something to do. He might be useful."

Fin remembered Liam, the Black Watch infantry soldier they'd met the same night they'd met Tam.

"Aye, we could use him. He should be able to take orders well enough."

"Where did you get this fucking van mate?" Liam asked Birt.

"I'm not your fucking mate, and it's my dad's old van, he used to be a market trader. I stole the plates off an abandoned car though and ground off all the serial numbers and all that shite," Birt said, happy as anyone Fin had ever seen.

"Market trader eh? You sure it runs? We can't have a breakdown or we'd be completely fucked," Fin said, looking dubiously at the rusty old heap of shite.

"No worries mate, no worries, I checked it over myself."
Birt's way with anything mechanical had got Fin out of no end of
shitty situations so he felt satisfied with that.

"Fine. Here's the plan boys … "

Edinburgh, Scotland, present day

"Hello?"

"Go down to the street and wait by the cafe across from
your office. Take a photographer. You have three minutes."

"Wait, what—" Click.

"Shit!" The reporter didn't need to think it through, he
recognised the voice from the wine bar. He sprinted from his
desk to Neil's, "Mate, get your camera, now!" Neil was a pro too,
his bag was packed and ready, he grabbed his 'ready' camera and
followed the rapidly disappearing reporter out the door.

Captain Reginald Dewhurst lost control of his bladder, then
began to blubber.

He wasn't a combat soldier—he was what Fin and other
soldiers from the 'teeth' end of the army referred to as a REMF, a
Rear-Echelon Mother Fucker. In his case, he was a logistics
officer, a pencil pusher.

For Fin he had made himself a target of opportunity by
simply walking down the street in uniform without close
protection. Things had seemed quiet to him, he'd just gone for
some scram.

Big mistake.

The boys had jumped him as he crossed an alley and he
found himself trussed and blindfolded in the back of a van before
he'd had time to think.

He'd caught a glimpse of his abductors and they looked like terrorists to him, with balaclavas and guns. He should have known better after the shootings in the city centre.

They stripped him down to his pants using sharp knives and he started blubbering and begging them not to kill him.

"We're not going to kill you ya stupid gash, now shut the fuck up before we change our mind." He snapped his mouth shut, but continued to whimper.

Then he felt them brushing him down with something cold and wet, making him squirm. That only earned him a sharp jab in the ribs, "Keep the fuck still arsehole, I don't want to fuck this up." He thought he heard someone stifle a giggle.

'Oh my God,' he thought, as they began cutting off his urine soaked pants.

A beat up blue transit van screeched to a halt about 100 metres away from the reporter.

"There Neil, there! Start shooting that van!"

The side door opened and a man staggered out. He looked like he was dressed all in blue. Neil's camera started clicking. The man staggered onto the pavement looking around dazed. They'd pulled a hood off him just as they'd pushed him out. His hands were tied behind his back. He was painted royal blue with white diagonal stripes from shoulders to hips.

The reporter started laughing, he couldn't help it, "He's a Scottish Saltire Neil! Brilliant!"

"Come on!" They sprinted up to the naked man, "You okay mate, what's your name?" Neil kept clicking away.

"Please call the police," voice shaking.

"No problem," then yelled to the nearest bystander, "someone call the police please!"

"Now, are you okay? Tell me your name."

"Dewhurst, Captain Reginald Dewhurst."

Bingo! The camera kept clicking and the reporter started composing headlines in his head.

Andy Skeen

Fire in the sky

Edinburgh, Scotland, present day

"Dewhurst! Who the fuck is Captain Dewhurst?"

Trentworth had had enough. Was the entire fucking army completely incompetent?

"Logistics Captain, Sir," his aid, Lieutenant Wilson replied, embarrassed. He was a former logistics officer.

"Anybody mind telling me why he was out walking around unaccompanied?"

"He, ah, went out for lunch sir."

After several moments of trying to regain his composure, Trentworth finally said, "Get me a line to the TCG in Hereford. I want action and I want it now or we're going to lose control of this situation."

"Right away sir."

Trentworth chewed his lip for a moment. The Special Regiments based out of Hereford could be compromised since many of the Scottish SF soldiers had gone AWOL, taking plenty of weaponry and other resources with them. They had to have had help. He needed outside help, people he knew he could count on. He'd never trusted the SAS or SBS and he wasn't going to start now.

"Belay that order Lieutenant. Please clear a secure line for me for a priority overseas call. I will dial direct. When I'm done with that, I will need to speak to the Prime Minister's office."

Heavy sheets of rain battered the roof of a small rusty blue van, doing the speed limit in a 20 zone, eased along a quiet farm lane a couple of miles from Edinburgh Airport. It slowed briefly near some woods where the streetlight had failed to come on that night—mainly because they had shot it out the night before with a suppressed rimfire rifle—then sped up again.

As the van slowed, Fin and Birt leapt from the van and rolled into the darkness under the shattered streetlight.

Both wore full sniper suits, but not just any sniper suits. They had night suits designed to defeat the infrared cameras mounted on the helicopters that were now patrolling the approaches to Edinburgh Airport. The army had set up a secure perimeter and suspended all flights except military flights for a few days, they said, at least until the situation stabilised. They'd diverted all civilian flights to Glasgow and set up what amounted to a ground and air forces operations centre.

Fin and Birt melted into the woods that flanked the stream and began their tactical advance. As they got within range of the perimeter, they went to ground, and began the belly crawl, stopping and checking with their NV goggles every ten metres.

They saw plenty of security at the fence, but nothing outside it. They'd dodged one patrol back on the road, but that was about it. Sloppy, or perhaps arrogant.

Fin checked the range finder, just under two klicks. Close enough. He began to look for somewhere to set up.

He found it, tucked into a hedgerow, with a perfect view of the runways and army staging areas. Three big fat army transport planes squatted in a nice neat row along the runway. The area appeared mostly quiet this late at night, but plenty of foot and vehicle patrols circled the airport perimeter.

"Range to the birds?"

Birt had already set up. "One-eight-two-four metres to bird one on the left, 40 more to bird two … another 40 to bird three. Wind steady right, 10kph, one quarter value."

"Roger that."

Fin filed that away and began unsheathing the big hammer, the US-made Barrett .50 calibre sniper rifle. Birt had already begun arranging magazines close at hand, each one colour coded for armour piercing, full-metal jacket and incendiary. They would light up the night, but try not to hurt anyone in the process.

They heard the sound of an approaching helicopter and quickly turned their heads to the ground and tucked their hands underneath them, hoping the thermal signature wouldn't give them away. It wouldn't if the suits did their job and the cold rain would certainly help too.

The chopper worked its was around the perimeter of the fields and wooded areas around the airport, getting closer and closer. They held themselves still and kept everything that could have a heat signature underneath their anti-thermal detection suits, faces in the dirt, with the hoods pulled up around their heads.

As the buzzing aircraft approached the two hidden men, it stopped and hovered.

"Hold there pilot," the officer monitoring the FLIR, the Forward Looking Infrared Radar, squawked into the young chopper pilot's ears. The pilot pulled smartly into an even hover. They'd been doing this all night, peering through the pouring rain at dogs, foxes and the occasional roe deer all around the airport. But that didn't deaden their heightened sense of threat. The intel and killings in town had seen to that.

"Strange, but it doesn't look human or animal though."

The other tech leaned over to get a look at the FLIR display and studied the grey smudge that appeared in a hedgerow that indicated something warm was there, or recently had, been.

"I've seen that before, it's an animal bed. A couple deer probably laid up there and got spooked off by our approach, that heat's just residual. Looks too cool to be anything else."

"Roger that, resume the patrol pilot."

The chopper had hovered for less than a minute, but it was enough to convince Fin and Birt they'd been made. Then it moved off and continued its patrol. They monitored all movement to see if it was just trying to convince them they'd not been seen, but nothing moved down at the airport and no extra patrols appeared in any direction. The chopper would complicate their exfiltration, but Birt had come up with an ingenious plan. It depended on impeccable timing.

"I think we're OK Birt, you still want to go ahead?"

"Roger that boss."

"I'm not your boss anymore Birt."

"You are when we're on an op boss." Fin caught a flash of Birt's smile and returned it. He felt good, being out on ops together again. Now it was just a matter of waiting and watching the clock. They would spend the time in close observation to make sure there were no personnel on the planes and judge the pattern of the security patrols.

"Military flight 475, you are cleared to land on runway delta x-ray".

Flight Commander Steve Marshall completed his turn over the Firth of Forth and lined up on Edinburgh's runway DX glowing in the distance. The computer said he would be on the ground in less than five minutes, first military flight of the day. He desperately needed a cup of coffee.

He'd already done this run a couple of times this week, dropping off more hardware and supplies to the growing operational forces on the ground. He'd done this same thing hundreds of times in Iraq and Afghanistan, but he couldn't get over the strangeness of doing it in Britain, of moving supplies only a few hundred miles north. They were on operational alert, but they weren't coming in dark or dropping chaff. The main threat was thought to be sabotage or small arms fire. So he kept his landing lights on and commenced his landing run.

Birt had been waiting. He watched as the big transport made its turn and lined up on the runway, coming in from their left.

"Here she comes boss, right on time."

"Roger that, I'm dialled. Where's that chopper."

"Southwest to our 2 o'clock, three klicks. The motor patrol has moved away and there are no guards or airport workers near the birds. You have a clear zone of fire. Range confirmed at one-eight-two-four metres to nearest bird. Wind steady right, 10kph, one-quarter value. Fire when ready."

Here he was again, settling into the world's biggest sniper rifle. Fin chambered a round from the mag he'd seated earlier, incendiary to start. He wanted to make a big show.

He didn't know whether the heavy transport jets would have full fuel tanks or not, he couldn't remember the procedure, but he knew they would have at least some fuel.

In less time than it took to finish his final breath, he ran a mental checklist of range against the adjustments he'd made and couldn't find a fault. He pushed his index finger through the slit in the finger of his glove and settled it gently against the trigger, taking up the slack.

He finished about half his exhale and paused, the crosshairs of the scope fixed firmly on the first transport's wing, right where the fuel tanks nestled inside.

Everything felt right. He relaxed and the crosshairs steadied as he gently brought pressure to the trigger. The sear broke perfectly, releasing the spring that held the firing pin, slamming it against the primer of the first round. The pin dented the primer, hammering the ignition element—the same stuff on the tip of a match—against a tiny internal anvil, heating it enough to ignite it, sending a flash of sparks into the body of the cartridge. That in turn set off about half a cup of highly engineered and shaped balls of gunpowder that sat inside the big brass case.

In less than an instant, the exploding powder created enough pressure inside the case, bound by the chamber of the rifle, to blast the sophisticated incendiary bullet down the bore. Precisely machined lands and grooves gripped the copper alloy jacket of the bullet as it slid down the barrel, imparting a stabilising spin to the lethal pointed projectile as it exited the barrel.

At nearly two kilometres, the bullet flight time gave Fin the seconds he needed to recover from the recoil and get his riflescope back on the target. He'd seen the hot glowing round flash upwards through his field of view on its arc-shaped trajectory to the target. Then he saw it fall back into view spot on target, puncturing the wing near the fuselage and detonating—just as it was designed to do.

A small explosion ripped open the wing, then a secondary explosion engulfed the entire midsection of the aircraft.

"Hit," Birt said automatically.

Fin pulled right and settled the crosshairs of the scope on the second plane.

Breath, trigger, release.

"Hit."

He didn't wait to see the results, his range was on. He adjusted the rifle.

Breath, trigger, release.

"Hit."

Three shots, three planes transformed into blazing infernos on the tarmac. No one killed as far as they could tell.

"Okay, let's get the fuck outta here."

They threw their gear together and began their quiet stalk back to the road. They heard the helicopter returning to investigate already. They could see the lights of the incoming transport aircraft on its final approach and knew they were directly under the flight path. Their timing had been perfect, the plane was committed and even if the tower waved him off at the last second, the chopper would have to steer clear of the flight path of the jet. They should have just enough time to get to the RV and exfil before the helicopter could locate them.

"What the hell!"

The chopper pilot spotted the erupting ball of orange at the airport and turned his bird to face it.

"They're here, they've fucking attacked the airport! Get over there, now!"

"Roger that."

The pilot swung around and jammed on the power, buzzing over burning planes into a sweeping search pattern on that side of the airport.

"Edinburgh tower to military Flight 457, abort landing, repeat abort landing. Acknowledge!"

"Flight 457 Edinburgh Tower, repeat last order, we are on final approach, over."

"We are under attack, abort, abort, abort."

"Roger that Edinburgh, aborting," the pilot responded calmly. He'd been here before in both Afghan and Iraq. "It's going to be close tower, we will buzz your airspace at less than 100 metres, over."

"Roger that, airspace will be cleared, over."

The pilot eased the controls back as hard as he dared, pouring on the power at the same time. He double-checked his altimeter and airspeed to see if they had enough altitude and power to make it out and decided they did.

"Edinburgh Tower to patrol aircraft Echo One, clear airspace immediately, we have inbound, over!"

"Negative tower, we are in pursuit of terrorists on the ground, wave them off, over."

"Echo One, this is not a request, you are in immediate danger of collision, over."

The young pilot's blood was up now and he didn't see the incoming transport, which was high, and out of his field of vision, but still coming down, not having levelled off yet. He scooted lower.

"I have them!" the tech shouted into the radio, "100 metres, dead ahead!"

The chopper had them, they were sure. They felt protected by the IR defeating suits, but the chopper would see movement as they sprinted across the open ground. It would also detect some heat from the hot barrel of the rifle if not much else. Fin decided to drop the heavy rifle.

Their exfil route took them straight across the approach to the main runway beneath the transport, but the patrol chopper had moved in anyway. At first Fin thought that maybe they'd mistimed their attack, but he could hear the roar of the engines to his right and knew the chopper would have to clear airspace or die.

They scurried in a half crouch along a hedge that ran across the runway approach. It would take then close to the RV point on a small lane east of the airport. The chopper suddenly flicked on its main spotlight, lighting them up like noon on a summer day, loudspeaker blaring, "Stop where you are or we will open fire!"

The transport pilot hadn't seen the chopper. Its flashing warning lights had blended into the background of airport and runway illumination, along with the inferno created by the three burning jets and the rain sluicing off the plane's windscreen. He had levelled off and begun to regain altitude at about 150 metres when the chopper turned on its spotlight only a few hundred metres directly in front of the nose of the massive jet.

With no time to think, the jet pilot just reacted. He wrestled the flight controls hard right against the chopper's direction of travel, poured on more power and prayed. With luck, they might just miss it.

Fin and Birt kept running. They could see the transport coming their way, nearly on top of then. The whining engines changed tempo as it wheeled to their left, away from the pursuing chopper coming up behind.

They dove into the ditch that ran next to the hedgerow, rolling onto their bergens to see what would happen.

The transport pilot had rolled the huge plane as far as he dared. The chopper pilot noticed the plane, now almost on top of him and jammed his stick over to bank hard to his right. For an agonising instant, they were aimed directly at each other, nose to nose, but their turns carried them apart.

They missed each other by less than 50 feet. The chopper pilot felt remarkably calm as he jerked his rudder right and surged the accelerator. The co-pilot had lost it though, "FUCK FUCK FUCK!"

The sharp bank was the first sign to the tech in the chopper that anything was wrong, with his eyes firmly on the FLIR monitor. The second was the terrified shouting of the co-pilot. Then the chopper's flight path took it directly into the jet wash of the transport's huge engines.

The wash pouring out of the four huge Rolls Royce turbine engines grabbed the chopper and flung it sideways into a wild spin. Everything went into slow motion as the pilot focused on holding the chopper level and stopping the spin, but he knew they were going down. His only hope was stopping the spin and taking the sting out of the impact. The jet pilot straightened out and began to gain altitude, wondering what the fuck had just happened.

As the jet missed the helicopter, Birt and Fin spotted the pick-up car coming up the lane. They jumped up and started running. They couldn't see what was happening behind them and didn't plan on stopping to find out. But they knew from the whine of the engine that the helicopter was coming down. The roar of the blades sounded like they were directly overhead, spurring them into a frantic sprint.

The chopper pilot managed to get the spin under control, but the craft was still bucking and the ground was coming up too fast. At the last, he thought he could see the terrorists on the ground below him, fleeing like rabbits under the spotlight. 'Well that's something,' he thought, 'at least we're going to crush the bastards.' Then everything went black.

The shock of the helicopter hitting the ground just a few metres behind them knocked them both off their feet. But it didn't explode. Fin glanced back and saw the face of the pilot in the glow of the instrument panel. He didn't look too bad. Fin hoped he would make it.

Within seconds they reached the RV and rolled into the open back of the farmer's Defender pickup. They burrowed into a pile of straw and cow dung. Fin thought he heard the mumbling of Punjabi prayers as they rolled off down the road.

Andy Skeen

Mercenary play day

BBC News

The military today reported that the operation to suppress terrorism in Scotland has made what they are calling significant advances. No details were released, but we have unofficial reports of raids and arrests by armed units all over Scotland.

The military authorities continue to seek Staff Sergeant Finlay McColl in connection with the Princes Street shootings, the attack at Edinburgh Airport and the abduction of an English officer.

Some people are calling Staff Sergeant McColl the new William Wallace, others say he's just a murdering terrorist, with opinion fractured along national lines. Earlier today I walked the streets of Stirling to ask the residents what they thought.

"It's terrible, all this violence, just terrible. We'll never gain independence if they keep this up, it will be just like Belfast, forever."

"—BEEP—ing English BEEP— s have it coming to ya aye? Go the BEEP home ya c—BEEP."

As you can see, passions are running high on both sides of the issue here. Back to you in London.

Edinburgh, Scotland, present day

A skate punk, swinging his board nonchalantly, watched the old beat-up telly in the main room of a run-down Leith pub while scratching his balls through his shorts. He tucked his board between his knees and reached for his pint, spilling some on his black anarchy t-shirt in the process.

If anybody noticed him at all, they might have thought he was a bit older than the average skater, but these days they came in all ages.

Luckily, the scene on the television held everyone's attention. A terrified British officer sat bound to a chair. No one in the pub said a word, they just stared and listened.

"Scottish terrorists have posted a video online and sent a link to several news outlets earlier today. It shows a kidnapped British officer, who has not yet been identified by the authorities. They spelled out their demands, number one of which is, quote, that the 'English army of occupation packs up and goes home.' There was nothing else with the video. Let's view the recording again."

Fin thought about scratching his balls again but thought that might be overplaying it a little, so he scratched his week old beard instead. He took another pull on his pint, savouring its cold bitterness.

On screen, two men in balaclavas stood either side of the officer with plenty of firepower on show. Only the officer spoke, reading a statement in a shaky pinched voice. "I have not been harmed, but they say they will kill me unless the English occupation force packs up and goes home. They say that you should know they are serious by what they've done on Princes Street and the Airport."

That's just like Jimmy. Taking credit for other people's work, Fin thought. He wondered if the little fuck would actually kill the officer in cold blood.

The newsreader continued, "In further dramatic news, the Prime Minister addressed Parliament today, declaring Martial Law in Scotland."

The screen showed the PM standing at the Despatch Box to complete silence in the House of Commons. "Honourable members, as of this moment, based on authority vested in me by His Majesty the King as Prime Minister of his Majesty's Parliament, I am declaring Martial Law in Scotland and putting Edinburgh directly under Military control. Checkpoints will be established on every road leading into and out of the city. I would ask that all citizens please bear with the authorities there and carry their passports with them at all times. General Edward Trentworth will remain in command and in control of Scottish civil and military administration. He will also continue to direct the operation against the Scottish terrorists. We are exploring every possible legal route to resolve this crisis, but as we do so, we cannot allow terrorists to undermine the peace and security of the entire nation."

Fin ground his teeth. His actions seemed to have just made things worse. The Prime Minister wasn't getting the message. He downed his pint in one and headed out, dropping his board loudly on the pavement before hopping aboard and kicking away.

Big Tam was working late. He'd spent the day clearing out the storage units that had been used by the SLA and Fin. They'd decided several days earlier that operational security required that they not stay anywhere more than a day or two.

A storage company had proved to be the perfect cover so far. Lots of people could come and go at all hours, moving large boxes and containers without anyone suspecting anything. The police knew Tam though. He'd been arrested before when a nationalist march had gotten out of hand. They hadn't charged him, but that didn't matter, they knew about him.

The Irish and the other hard cases had disappeared with Jimmy the night of the independence vote. Now it looked like they'd well and truly gone rogue.

Tam had started entering an invoice when the large plate glass window of his office exploded inwards and two ninjas with submachine guns burst through.

He knew what to do and threw his hands straight in the air. They were on him immediately, shouting "Clear!" so their comrades would know the room was secure. They threw him face down on the glass-ridden floor, one put a boot on his head and ground his cheek into the glass while the other plasti-cuffed his wrists behind his back.

They dragged him out the door by his elbows to a waiting military Land Rover and tossed him like a sack of potatoes into the back.

'Not police then,' Tam thought, wondering just who the hell these guys were and exactly what the day's declaration of Martial Law meant in terms of his rights, or if he had any left at all. He could hear them tearing his business to pieces with crowbars and blowtorches. He hoped he and his men had been thorough enough and hadn't left any traces. The other members of his SLA cell had gone into hiding, dividing up the materiel among them to cache it away.

"It's going to be easier if you tell us what you know now. We're under martial law now Big Tam," the black clad man said, smirking behind his balaclava. "Do you know what that means?"

"About what? I don't know anything about anything."

"Look knob-head, I've got orders, and those orders are to extract the information we require. Understand? No one but us knows you're here. No official body has our names or knows this unit is operating on Scottish soil. Do you hear what I'm saying? This isn't going to go well for you son."

That's how it was then. Fin had warned him that he thought Trentworth was capable of just about anything—here was the proof.

"If that's the case you'll never let me go anyway right?"

"We don't want to kill you chum, we're both British right?"

"Maybe, but thank fuck I'm not an English cunt like you."

He didn't see the fist coming, but he sure felt it, and heard the crunching of his nose cartilage as it struck. Losing his temper probably wasn't the wisest thing he'd ever done, he thought, as another fist slammed into his ribs.

Tom, the farmer who owned the safe house that Tam had sent them to, sauntered into the barn in a blue boiler suit and Wellington boots and started speaking to Fin and Birt without preamble, "They're searching all SIP members and picking up all known hard-core separatists and SLA members, everyone. They stormed Tam's place this morning. You boys best be on your way."

They had already prepared, but dodging checkpoints and patrols in broad daylight wouldn't be easy. And they didn't have anyplace to go.

"I got this today, by carrier pigeon."

Fin grinned, pure genius. He couldn't get over the fact that the farmer actually used pigeons to communicate with the resistance that seemed to have sprung out of nowhere.

"The leadership says those Irish boys, and their pals who are calling themselves the Real SLA, have killed that hostage. They have information that those wackos might be planning something big, really big and really stupid. You've got to try and stop it if you can before things get worse. Here's an address of an abandoned house where we think they're holed up, and here's the address of a clean safe house, someone not known to the police. Don't eat her cooking though, you've been warned. They'll get more information to you there."

The former First Minister of Scotland sat watching the news, his face grim. He was beginning to lose hope that the situation could be resolved and he blamed himself for everything. Who could have known the English would overreact so badly? Martial Law! How could he have misjudged them so?

And now they were reporting that these 'Real' SLA nut cases had killed their hostage to "make a point."

His only hope now was to use what little influence he had to save his beautiful country. One of his only means of contact with the outside world was now by carrier pigeon. When the military figured that out, if they ever did, he wondered what they would think.

Under house arrest at his Morningside home, mobile phone confiscated, rarely left alone, he spent his time watching the news and tending his pigeons, and those his oldest friend and shooting partner Tom had left with him. They'd shared a love of homing pigeons, as both their fathers kept them and had also been lifelong friends. He trusted Tom without any reservation.

The pigeons would go straight home and Tom would know what to do.

He wasn't completely without resources. MI5 and the UK Civil Service contained many a sympathetic Scot who had stayed in their positions. For decades he had cultivated relationships with them through his time in government and the SIP.

They all had ways of contacting him and helping him. They were his only hope of helping Scotland avoid a decades-long blood bath of the type that had afflicted Ireland. His contacts included a cadre of loyal SIP members and a pair of incredibly brave and apparently loyal SAS men. And one of them was a Sikh, imagine that! He knew they weren't the killers. Tom had been keeping an eye on them. He was beginning to trust them completely. Their operation at the airport had been spectacular and not a soul had been harmed.

A uniformed soldier, taking a rest from eating the First Minister's biscuits, poked his head into the lounge. He didn't say a word, just stared at the apparently placid politician who ignored him and watched the news about the discovery of the mutilated body of the kidnapped British officer.

The soldier finally spoke, losing his cool, "Fucking scum." He turned and walked away without letting on if he meant the killers or McAdam.

"We've got something boss!"

'Shit,' Tam thought, 'what had they overlooked?'

"Storage container 135B, guns, det cord, timers, even some Iraqi RPGs!"

Tam couldn't believe it. Who the fuck? Then it dawned on him what he'd overlooked. Jimmy's sister. She'd rented a unit from him years ago when their mother had passed on.

This could work in his favour, he could give them Jimmy!

"All right arsehole, what the fuck do you know about this? I want to know who's fucking storage unit this was, when they were last here and whether they fold or fucking crumple the bog roll when they wipe the shit from their arse. Do you get me?"

"No problem, I'll tell you everything I know, no problem." Tam gave a great impression of being shaken and scared after they'd roughed him up. Now he'd start naming names of people in Jimmy's faction. Perfect. "Take me to my computer, I'll show you everything I have."

In his office he looked up the records and printed them off while the three men stood over him, closely watching everything he did.

"Yes, I know this woman. I think it's her brother you're after, a guy named Jimmy. Same last name I think, the woman never married. He's a soldier and a bit wild. I know some of his mates, they're all a bit crazy if you ask me. I mean, I'm a nationalist right, but these boys are scary. There was some Irish fuckers with them too, covered with tats." With that, he named everyone who had left that night with Jimmy.

"What about Staff Sergeant Finlay McColl and Sergeant Sabjirt Singh?"

"Never heard of them."

His interrogator turned back to one of the other men guarding the room, "Call in what we have so far, while I let old Tam here try to convince me he's not a fucking liar."

A left and right

Stirlingshire, north of Edinburgh, Scotland, present day

A car had appeared for them, sitting in the drive, keys in the ignition. A plain black hatchback, but it had a good engine and sporty tyres. They rolled away from the farm quietly and without any fanfare. Tom nodded at them as they left and carried on with his unending chores.

"I don't know what I'm going to tell my father mate." Desperate times called for desperate measures and Birt had made an extreme sacrifice. He cut his hair. Like most religious Sikhs he'd never cut his hair and kept it twisted tightly into a turban or other hair covering to keep it under control. But a Scot and a Sikh travelling together in a car would be a sure ticket to capture or worse.

Fin knew it bothered him, but it had been Birt's idea.

"Well, I'm sure he'd prefer that you didn't end up dead or in prison pal."

"Hmmh."

Both had shaved and scrubbed up, then put on some business suits. Fin had dyed his hair blond too, now that it had grown in a little.

"How much do these suits costs again Birt?"

"Never mind mate, just don't fuck yours up, right?"

Fin grinned back at him.

"Where we going then?" Birt asked.

"Another farm in Stirlingshire, but I have something I need to do before we go out there. It's on the way."

They managed to dodge patrols and remained undetected leaving the Lothian area by using a cut through and a farm track. It didn't do the car's suspension any good, but they got out clean.

Heading north, they approached the town of Stirling with its imposing castle on an extinct volcano that seemed to burst out of an otherwise flat landscape. Fin smirked as they passed by the site of the Battle of Bannockburn, his sense of irony tingling.

He turned off the main road soon after, entering a winding track that led to the top of another imposing hill that had a huge stone monument on top. The massive stone monument and museum to William Wallace.

Every Scot knows the story of the great hero William Wallace and likewise knows how ridiculous the movie was. Still, the movie stands as a symbol and they play a clip of Mel Gibson painted for battle and wielding a replica of William Wallace's famous claymore on the massive screens at every international sporting match, especially when Scotland plays England in anything. And every time the arenas erupt in deafening passion.

"What's this about Fin? You getting delusions of something mate?"

"Fuck no, you skinny shite, just wanted to see it again. Think about him."

"You're not William Wallace boss."

"No shit. I'm not worthy to wipe his arse. But I'm a son of his legacy and … I thought I might find something."

Birt elected to keep quiet at that and followed along a bit puzzled at this turn of sentimentality in his normally quiet stoic boss. They looked at Wallace's huge claymore sword, then climbed to the top of the tower to view the area of his greatest triumph at Bannockburn. Fin stared at both for a long time, saying nothing. He was thinking about Wallace's fate, betrayed by Scots, horrifically killed at the Tower of London before being dismembered and having parts of his body put on display around England.

Fin wandered down, Birt following quietly behind to stare at the stone statue out front, before someone—maybe a tourist, maybe not—stopped dead and looked at him, then hurriedly walked on.

"Time to go boss," Birt said.

"Yep."

They walked nonchalantly to their car and got in, driving away as if nothing was wrong. They headed in the opposite direction from the safe house at the bottom, in case the man was still watching. They circled back to check their tail, but they hurried knowing that they'd have a chopper here soon.

They had an operation to plan and they needed to stop Jimmy from whatever he was going to do. Tom had said they'd get more information at the next safe house.

"There's something here for you."

Iain, the tough mechanic who owned the tractor repair centre they were hiding out at handed them an unaddressed envelope.

"Who's it from?"

"Not a clue."

"How did it get here?"

"I'm not to say, just hand it over."

Birt took the envelope and opened it while Fin looked on. It held a single piece of paper with a typed message. It contained the code word they'd been given to show that it came directly from the First Minister. It had all the information they needed.

"We need a couple cars."

"On road or off?"

"Bit of both maybe, untraceable to you would be best."

The mechanic pursed his lips, "Tomorrow morning soon enough?"

"Perfect, we have some thinking to do."

Early the next morning the mechanic handed them the keys to two cars in the forecourt, a small white van and a beat up farmer's Land Rover. Perfect.

"Here's the name and address of two other safe houses, one in the Borders, one in East Lothian. Memorise them, then throw these away, right?"

"Yep, we know the drill, thanks mate," Fin began to turn away.

"Mr. McColl?"

Fin turned back a bit surprised, the chap had never given any indication that he knew who they were.

"Aye?"

"Did you kill those men on Princes Street?"

"No. No I did not. I'm going to stop someone who is going to kill more."

"Scotland must be free Mr. McColl."

"Yes, she must."

"Don't you think that if they won't let us go, that we should do what needs to be done?"

Fin couldn't think of what to say. God knows he'd "done what needed to be done" to enough people in enough countries that he certainly had no place taking the moral high ground.

"We're not there yet pal, we really aren't. And if we keep going down this route, Scotland will turn into a hellhole like Northern Ireland or Afghanistan, with criminal gangs, violence and death for years to come. Do you want your children to grow up in that world?"

The mechanic just stared, resentful and angry, not willing to listen.

"I did the Airport job and made a fool of that English officer, but I won't kill anyone. I just want them to get the message and back down. But we have to stop the Real SLA or we're going to be screwed. Got it?"

"Whatever you say. But Scotland must be free."

This exchange added to Fin's sense of urgency. Every day they inched closer to a real blood bath, to real terrorism. This guy looked like a prime recruit and there must be hundreds like him, getting angrier and angrier as they saw the army on the streets. Centuries old resentments had flared from a smouldering ember to a roaring flame that could burn Scotland, and England, to the ground. Anyone who had lived through the troubles knew what that meant, dead children on the streets of London and Manchester.

The clock was ticking and he knew he had to do something if he could.

Edinburgh, Scotland, present day

Birt walked along an Edinburgh side street, dressed in whites and an apron, with a food services hat on. He smirked at himself, thinking that he was a walking fucking cliché, just another south Asian curry house worker out on his break. He carried a box he'd picked up out behind just such an establishment, the smells of hot Indian food making his stomach growl. Punjabi script covered the box, with a graphic of a bunch of peppers. He carried the box on his shoulder, like he was on his way back to his restaurant.

The chubby reporter picked up the phone on the first ring, "What?!"

"Go have a cigarette pal"—click.

It was him, McColl. No time for thought, he jumped up and headed downstairs. Since the smoking ban came into effect in Scotland, all smoking took place outside. At first it took place in the front of the building until the non-smokers whinged about the smoky haze that enveloped the front entrance. Now it took place behind the building in an alley, where the smells from the back door of a nearby curry house tortured growling stomachs daily.

He pushed into the alley, trying to look casual. No one there except a guy from the curry house. He thought he'd seem him there before. As he liberated a Marlboro from the pack and flicked on his light the cook walked over, grinning a bit, fake waiter smile, "Got a light mate? Left mine inside."

Briefly taken aback by the Glaswegian accent, the reporter fumbled a bit, then flicked the lighter, lighting the cigarette himself, deciding it would be rude not to, afraid the guy would think he was a racist if he just handed over the lighter. Then chided himself for being such silly arse and wished he didn't have to think about that shit, that they could just be a couple a guys having a smoke, wondering if the other guy felt the same way, wishing he could ask without being an arse.

Fuck it. The Asian broke the silence for him.

"You're that reporter eh? From the paper, but on the telly too eh??

"Yeah mate, that's me."

"Sound mate, sound. I've got a message for you. Look at my face. You know me?"

Confused, he just stared stupidly, then it dawned on him. Fuck me, Sabjirt Singh!

Birt saw the dawning recognition, "Good, now listen closely, I'm giving you a chance at something, you decide. Do you want to take a ride? See something? Could be a bit dicey mate. You can always make out we kidnapped you later to stay out of trouble. All we ask is that you tell the truth about what you see. You in? Story of your life mate. Maybe a book, whatever. Decide now."

Hell yes he was in.

"I'm in. What do you need me to do."

"We leave now, no going back to your desk. Please give me your phone."

He sighed, no chance to call in, nothing, but he thought it would be worth it. If these guys wanted to hurt him, they'd have done it long ago. He pulled it out and handed it over.

"You got your wallet on you? Keys?"

"Yes".

"Good, no reason to go back to your desk. Our ride will be here shortly." Birt held up his phone, showing that it had been on the whole time. No doubt McColl was on the other end of that call, listening in.

A white van turned into the alley gliding to a stop, "Get in front."

And they were off.

"Sir, we don't think the person doing the killing is McColl, we think it's one Jimmy McLeod. An SAS staff sergeant. Sir, McLeod's file says he is an explosives expert.."

"What are you talking about? McColl was spotted fleeing the scene."

"We have some new intel and we believe it. We think McColl did the Dewhurst kidnapping and didn't kill him. We also think he did the Airport operation when no one got hurt. That was him, pure sniper, two klicks out with a .50-cal. We've also determined that there were two shooters on Princes Street, shooting different rifles. Only one was shooting a .50-cal, and it only shot up vehicles. Someone else did the shooting that killed the officers with a standard issue .338 Lapua. Sir, we think there's a rift in the SLA between moderate and more extremist elements. Sir, the extremist faction includes Irish dissident Republicans."

"Give me the intel. I'll decide for myself."

With that, the officer showed him the detailed reports and recounted what Tam had told his men about Jimmy McLeod. He'd given up all his known associates and they checked out. They'd made more arrests, found weapons, but no mention of Fin McColl.

"Sir, some of those arrested laughed when McColl's name was mentioned. They called him a coward and a poof. They said he didn't have the balls to do what needed to be done. By the way sir, most of them have gone on a hunger strike."

'Just what we fucking need,' Trentworth thought. He only partially bought the story. "Fine, focus your line of inquiry on Jimmy, but don't let up on McColl. I know that bastard, he is capable of killing in cold blood. Just like his bastard of a father."

"All right McDuff," Fin said to the reporter deliberately getting his name wrong as usual, "You go where we say, do what we say and you'll be fine. If you do anything else, chances are you will get yourself hurt. Get me?"

"Yes," the reporter replied. He'd barely said a word since they'd picked him up, just taking it all in, taking pictures, making short videos and notes as they'd prepared.

McColl, Singhe and a nameless youngish Scot who didn't say a word, returned the favour. McColl had simply told him to keep his mouth shut and take as many pictures as he wanted, he would answer questions later.

He'd watched while they all stripped and cleaned weapons, from a big sniper rifle to one small machine pistol and a handgun each. Then they'd strapped on their weaponry, covering it with plain white boiler suits.

After that, they took him out behind the barn they were staying in and did a very strange thing. They mixed up some wall plaster in a wheelbarrow. Singhe had started it by slinging some plaster at McColl, who slung some back. This touched off a no-holds barred plaster fight, which included McDougal. When it was done, they were all covered with plaster, including their faces and hair.

"Right, luckily, it's sunny, time for a little nap," and with that, they'd lain out in the sun for half an hour, letting the plaster dry a bit.

"Okay, now we need to make it look like we've made an effort to get this off, but not too much."

Very soon they all looked just like a team of plasterers just come off a job.

"Liam, get the kettle on, would you pal? I'm going to fill in McDougal here on what we think is going to happen tonight, " Fin said, gesturing to the plump reporter.

"Roger that Staff." McDougal found it fascinating that 'Liam' continued to refer to McColl as 'Staff', short for 'Staff Sergeant.' Obviously he was a soldier too, just as the reporter had guessed.

"Two and moo for me private!" Singhe had called after the retreating Liam, demanding two sugars with milk in his tea.

McColl spoke first, waiting for McDougal to flick on his tiny digital video camera. "We think that some very bad men are going to try to blow up something tonight. Their leader is the same man who did the killing on Princes Street and who killed that officer. I have no trouble telling you his name now, James McLeod. They call him Jimmy. We were in the SAS together. He's … he was … our bomb man. He blows shit up and he's damned good at his job."

"How do you know?"

"Sorry, I can't tell you that. What I can tell you is that he's going to do it tonight and that he's an evil bastard. We haven't killed anyone. We're just trying to send a message that it's time for the English to go home. I think this guy enjoys killing. Professional soldiers do it because they have to. It's their job. No pleasure, no remorse. I think Jimmy's different. Our last operation was worse than usual, you get me?"

"Why don't you tell the authorities he's coming?" Liam asked.

"First, they're not the rightful authorities here. Second, we don't know exactly where he's going to strike, just a vague idea. Third, I seriously doubt they could deal with this guy. He's good, one of the best explosives guys in the Regiment and a good sniper."

Birt in his role as spotter, and given his head for operational details, meant he usually did the planning. Fin always wondered why he hadn't tried for a commission, but when he asked Birt had just smiled and said he'd miss going on ops. He was an enlisted man's enlisted man, not wanting to give up on the excitement of front line operations in return for the privilege of rank. Besides, rank got a little blurry in the Regiment sometimes, with Birt having plenty of opportunity to contribute to operational planning as well as execution.

"So the intel we have, probably from someone who got cold feet, is that Jimmy is going to try to kill Trentworth using a roadside IED. He's the best in the business at that kind of shit so we have to take it seriously."

Liam raised his hand like a school boy, "Sergeant Singhe, if the intel is from a traitor won't they know and call it off?"

"The orders we have say that it's going to happen tonight, which means that the info was probably delivered to a member of the SLA without the Real SLA guys knowing about it. Guy's probably had a change of heart, but is scared shitless of the Irish boys. Any more questions?"

Liam shook his head, "No sergeant."

"Good, now stop fucking calling me sergeant pal. Call me Birt. Now, Trentworth leaves the Exec building between 18:00 and 20:00 hours, travelling in a hardened executive car in a small security convoy. He never takes exactly the same route to his secure quarters at the army grounds in the south of the city. But one section is always the same. When the convoy leaves the underground car park, he has to turn left or right."

Birt pulled open a commercial map of Edinburgh, spreading it out on the bench. "For about a hundred metres in either direction, he has no options, he has to follow this route. They think that Jimmy will hit him along that section. We simply don't know where the bomb will be. What we do know is that Jimmy will need line of sight."

McDougal spoke up, "Don't you think we should warn Trentworth? Seriously."

Fin answered, "What it comes down to McDougal, is that I want the RSLA out of action. This is our chance. It's a risk, but if we warn Trentworth, Jimmy won't be vulnerable and we can't take him out. He'll just bide his time and do something else, maybe hurt innocent civilians instead of going after Trentworth, who is military and therefore a legitimate target."

Birt wondered if Fin was going to save Trentworth so he could kill him himself. Or if he was just going to let Jimmy kill him.

Birt continued, "He will need line of sight, so what we're going to do is set up here," indicating a point on the map, "It's an abandoned house that offers a good view of the area. I think it will give us the best chance of spotting Jimmy and taking him out, or locating the bomb and taking it out."

Liam raised his hand again. "Sergeant," he said, earning a wry grin from Birt, "what am I here for?"

"You are site security. You're going to stay on the ground floor of the house with the door open. Walk in and out of the house to the van parked out front, mixing plaster and that sort of shit. Stay alert, make yourself some tea and generally look like a lazy plasterer."

"And me?" McDougal asked.

"You're with us. We'll be on binoculars and spotting scopes. We'll be looking for the bomb and Jimmy. You've got a front seat to whatever the fuck is going to happen, so you can report it. Let's get loaded up and get in place."

An hour later, McDougal watched as Fin and Birt set up. They each chose different windows on the same corner, pointed 90 degrees away from each other. Both had massive spotting scopes set up, back from the windows. They each also had a powerful set of binoculars and had given him a pair,

Birt grinned at the plump sweaty reporter, "Just stay back from the fucking windows right? Jimmy will also have security and be looking for us, and there are probably army snipers on the exec building. We'll make sure you don't miss anything. Got it?"

"Got it. What are you doing now?"

"First we're going to see if we can locate the bomb. It should be along that section of street there, from that corner to that corner. We've got at least a couple hours. Fin is going to try to locate Jimmy, but that will be harder. He could be in disguise, in a hide or on a high point somewhere that has line of site to the street so that he can detonate at the right moment."

"What's that for?" indicating an odd looking rifle.

"That is a suppressed sniper rifle. How much detail do you want?" His signature on the Official Secrets Act was the least of his worries so fuck it, he'd tell the guy everything.

"Everything, I'll filter it out later."

"It's a simple 7.62 calibre sniper rifle with a few tweaks. First, it has this," pointing at a two-foot long sleeve that fitted down over the barrel and screwed on, "a baffled can that contains the muzzle blast and dampens the sound. I've got two kinds of ammo. One is subsonic, which means that it doesn't break the sound barrier when it leaves the barrel. It's about as loud as a handclap if it's used with a sound moderator. The other is a normal full-power accuracy round. I can change the setting on my scope for either round, any distance out to about 300 metres for the subsonic round and about 800 for the full power round. I want to be silent if possible and get us the fuck out of here safely if I can."

"You're going to shoot Jimmy?"

"Maybe, I'd prefer to try to disable the bomb if we can locate it."

An hour later, his excitement had worn off, his sweat had dried and McDougal was starting to get bored. Fin and Birt had sat down and hadn't really moved much in all that time. They simply sat there and looked through their spotting scopes, adjusting them and moving them in tiny increments.

At first the reporter had stood behind them and searched himself. That had lasted about twenty minutes, before he'd sat down and made more notes for his story, bringing his notebook up to date on what they'd done so far. He'd taken a bunch of pictures of the boys at their spotting scopes and of the suppressed sniper rifle. He also took a few shots out the windows over the boy's heads, but mindful of what Birt had said about the windows. Then he'd gone down stairs to see what Liam was up to. The young private had set up what looked like a convincing plastering operation in the front garden, where he mixed plaster and brought it inside in buckets. He'd even started plastering a section of exposed brickwork. It wouldn't stand up to any sort of scrutiny, but McDougal would have been convinced by it. He took a few more pictures.

The young soldier had ignored him, so he went back up stairs. Just as he entered the sitting room, the window in front of Fin exploded inwards, and Fin hit the floor.

"Holy shit!" the reporter shouted standing there with his mouth open.

"Get down!" Birt also fell to the floor and started crawling towards Fin.

Fin was fine, "I'm good mate, he missed, or the glass deflected the shot. Just a cut on my face I think."

"Was that a shot?! What happened? Is that Jimmy?!" the reporter started babbling. Both Fin and Birt recognised the terror that went with being shot at for the first time, they'd both experienced it.

Birt answered, "Yes, he's spotted us, LIAM! STAY INSIDE NOW!"

Liam's voice floated up, "Roger that!"

"I think I know where he is," Fin said.

"Too late for that mate, he knows where you are. I think we're safe over here, and I think I have the bomb."

They moved carefully to the window, peeking out, "See the rubbish bins, two of them? One on each of the two possible routes?"

"Got 'em." They didn't need to speak, Fin just edged around the side of the room towards the table where his rifle was, then lunged forward and grabbed it. A thud and a hole in the table announced that Jimmy was still watching, still had his scope trained on the window. He too was shooting a suppressed rifle.

"What? I don't get it?" the reporter asked, but having enough presence of mind to keep taking pictures.

"They removed all the rubbish bins along the route days ago and they weren't there when I scouted this position yesterday. I compared them with the photos I took. It shouldn't have taken me an hour to figure it out, but you know what they say about hiding in plain sight. If they can fool me, they can fool Trentworth's security." Birt said, looking chagrined.

"Why is there two?"

"Jimmy's got both options covered, whichever way Trentworth goes, he gets the good news. Whatever's in those bins is going to be enough to take out a hardened security car. But even if it doesn't it will certainly send the kind of message Jimmy wants sending, that he's coming for the English leadership."

The reporter looked on as Fin settled the rifle on a table, held up by a bipod, set back from the window. Then snugged up to it and began to focus on his breathing. He used a small beanbag under the heel of the stock to get a steadier rest.

Birt already had the bins ranged, "Nearest target is two-two-five metres, the other is two-eight-five metres. Wind is minimal, target area is clear. Fire at will.

Fin exhaled and pulled the trigger, jacking the bolt and kept on firing. He cleared the ten round magazine, then put in another magazine and put ten more down range. Only someone standing near the bins would have noticed the thunk of the bullets and the holes appearing in the side of each, ten in each bin. Fin just hoped it would be enough. The bombs didn't explode, like in the movies, he was just trying to disable them.

Whoever was on the other end of the sniper rifle noticed and started putting rounds into the building, with bullets thwacking into the floor and walls behind the window. Luckily they were in a solid brick building. It would take more than whatever the sniper was shooting to penetrate it.

"Fin look!" Birt pointed to where the building on the side of the exec building was opening. Trentworth was coming out. McDougal started shooting pictures.

Two black Land Rovers came out first, pausing at the end of the ramp, while the security took a look around. Four men sat in each, two up, two back. The two in back had CQB carbines on their chest. It looked like there were more men in the back of each vehicle. One turned left and the other right, driving slowly.

"They've upgraded security," Birt said, "They've got a decoy."

"Liam! Get ready to go, start the van!"

"Roger that!"

The Jaguars with blacked out windows came out, one turning left, one right, each speeding up to take its position behind the security vehicles. Each in turn was followed by another Land Rover filled with men, making two convoys of three vehicles each.

They held their breath, hoping Fin had done enough to render the bomb inoperable, McDougal snapped pictures.

The convoy on the right reached its bin first and each vehicle cruised past without incident and its security didn't notice that the bin shouldn't be there.

The first vehicle of the second convoy reached the bin and moved past. When the second vehicle, the Jag, reached the bin, it exploded. A huge fireball engulfed the Jag, it had obviously been a shaped charge, perhaps with molten copper projectiles. The impact flipped the Jag over on its roof where it sat burning. The reporter kept snapping.

"Look!" The other convoy sped away, while security men in the bombed convoy poured out instinctively and set up a perimeter around the burning Jag.

"Trentworth's in the other Jag or they wouldn't be fucking off."

Fin edged quickly towards the other window, peeking through it. Looking at the window he thought Jimmy was hiding behind, he thought he saw a curtain twitch. He jumped down, crawled around to get behind his rifle, then popped up and slammed it to his shoulder, searching for the window and quickly found it. The curtain twitched again, then widened further and he saw binoculars. Definitely one of them, probably Jimmy, and not someone's grandmother.

He pressed the trigger. The suppressor took away most of the recoil and he rode what little there was to see the binoculars flip back out of the open window. He'd gone for a temple shot. He just hoped his aim was true. Whatever anyone thought, the security men in the decoy vehicle below hadn't deserved to die. Trentworth, maybe, but those boys were just doing their job.

"Time to go."

They left everything except their personal weapons and binoculars, sprinting down the stairs and into waiting van. The security cordon couldn't see them from this side so they were safe for the moment, at least until the police responded. McDougal had his precious camera and notebook.

They cruised away, doing their best to look like plasterers, talking and laughing. Fin didn't feel like laughing though. He could have warned them and no one would have died today, it was his fault. And he didn't feel great about killing Jimmy, if he had killed Jimmy. They'd shared a lot of whisky and risked life and limb together for years. They guy was a crazy fucker, but they'd been comrades in arms.

"Fuck it."

McDougal looked at him, "You all right McColl?"

"That wasn't exactly what I had in mind, but I think Trentworth is safe. I also think I got Jimmy. What are you going to write?"

"I'm just going to tell the story. I believe you. Take me to my office, the editor will still be there. He'll make me call the police, but not before I download the contents of my camera and rough out the story."

They pulled up in the alley behind the newspaper and left him by the back door.

"Right boys, we need to split up from here, things are going to get a lot worse I think. Liam, take us to where we dropped the other cars."

> ### BBC News – Breaking News
>
> *'We're getting reports that the Interim Governor of Scotland, Brigadier General Edward Trentworth, has narrowly escaped an assassination attempt.*
>
> *'Just before 8pm this evening, an improvised explosive device went off next to his vehicle just after it exited the Scottish Executive Building in the north of Edinburgh.*
>
> *'The pictures you're seeing are live, showing a burning vehicle near the building, but officials have confirmed that Governor Trentworth is alive and will meet with the press shortly. We will keep you informed as further details become available.'*

Andy Skeen

A cold drink of water

McDougal's story made the front page next to a large picture of Fin and Birt dressed as plasterers and heavily armed. The headline read, "Our New William Wallaces?"

The inside spread had numerous photos of Fin, Birt and Liam preparing for the operation. It also included a detailed map and diagram showing the location of the two convoys, where the boys had set up and where Jimmy had been. The story included news that Jimmy McLeod's body had been discovered.

The security forces declined to comment, saying that the investigation was ongoing. It detailed the efforts that Fin had put into disabling the bombs and neutralising Jimmy, with McDougal saying that he had seen the bullet holes in the two bins and knew they'd tried their best. He wrote about Fin's contrition that he hadn't warned the security forces, admitting that it was a mistake made in his zeal to neutralise the RSLA.

For the first time, Scotland and England learned of the split in the SLA, with Jimmy and his crew calling themselves the Real Scottish Liberation Army, and including assertions by Fin McColl that the Real and/or Provisional IRA had become involved. The story also quoted Fin describing what happened on Princes Street the night of the Declaration of Scottish Independence. Fin was also quoted expressing his apology to the helicopter crew at the airport, his relief that they'd survived and wishing them well as they recovered from their crash.

Within hours, Fin and Birt became national heroes and legends. Blogs and social media sites sung their praises throughout Scotland and the world, true modern freedom fighters who didn't want to hurt anyone.

Rural location east of Edinburgh, Scotland, present day

The snatch team had been raiding known activists and SLA sympathisers for days. They were getting down to the dregs now. Little grannies' two bedroom flats in the suburbs, pensioners in council houses, anyone and everyone who'd had anything to do with Scottish independence had been visited, some calmly, others with body armour and shouting.

Today was another such day, a small farm in East Lothian. Mainly wheat in the low fields and some sheep on rolling heather-covered hills. Colin Mowat and his wife had been active in the local party for 25 years, since taking over the farm from her father. In all respects they seemed like fine law-abiding citizens, but the team still had to check.

Records showed that the farmer had firearm and shotgun certificates for dealing with agricultural pests. So they'd decided to go in heavy, just to be safe.

The loft provided a warm and comfortable billet for Birt. Fin had demanded that they split up after the latest drama in Edinburgh, as they were too vulnerable and recognisable together. He'd sent Birt on to the East Lothian safe house to lie up for a few days.

He was snoozing lightly when something just felt wrong. Dogs barking. Could be foxes or even deer.

Quiet birds. Too early for their morning song?

No, something was definitely wrong.

He eased out of his bunk and moved to the window. There they were, a full entry team, maybe five guys, plus a perimeter team. No way out, it was hide, fight or give up. He rubbed his chin with his thumb.

He did as Fin instructed. He gave himself up. No sense in getting himself killed, or more importantly, getting the nice elderly farming couple hurt or their property damaged.

He walked down the loft ladder and went into the kitchen to make himself a cup of tea. He'd just taken the first sip when the team burst into the back door.

Edinburgh, Scotland, present day

"I know you've been through the training and we won't break you easily so let's get right to the point. We are not SAS or you'd know us right? Who do you think we are?"

Birt didn't recognise their voices for sure, nor their equipment. He thought they might be mercenaries, like those we saw so often in Iraq and Afghanistan.

"Can I have a glass of water." He kept a straight face, looking straight down at the table, not engaging his captors in any way. He thought he heard someone chuckle.

"You are off the grid now boy, blacker than black. No one knows we have you, it's down to you and me. I suppose we could go after your family, maybe bring your cute little niece here. Make you watch while we show her a good time. What is she, thirteen? Ripe mate, ripe."

Birt just played the grey man, quiet, nothing to say, limp in his chair.

"As much fun as that would be, we just don't have time for it. Shall I give you a choice? Water board or electricity? Hey? Which one do you fancy?"

Birt just stared at the table, slack jawed, vacant stare.

"Well boys, let's give our friend a drink of water then, shall we?"

He put up no resistance, just went limp as they blindfolded him and dragged him into another room. He felt them strapping him down to a hard table or something and thought he could he water dripping or sloshing around behind him. Water board then. He knew he could only beat it by accepting the inevitability of death. It comes to everyone in the end, maybe this was his time. But he couldn't stop himself, as they began to drown him, he began to fight.

Only, he didn't know anything. They'd split up, he didn't know where Fin was, and Fin didn't know where he was. In his mind he knew he was not necessarily in any great danger, these guys were experienced operators, they wouldn't let him die. But he still couldn't fight the waves of panic that instinctively accompany drowning.

The small bit of him that thought he was going to be okay suddenly decided that something was very wrong, Water had flooded his lungs, too much. He couldn't get any air and couldn't cough it out. He began to fight the bonds that held him, arching his back and choking, then he vomited.

He went limp in weakness, then lost consciousness.

"What the fuck?! Get him off the board, he's drowning goddamnit! Get him off!"

They pulled him to the floor and began life saving drills, but his breathing had stopped, then his heart stopped. Sabjirt Singhe, of a long line of great warrior heroes, had died helpless and among enemies, drowned, covered in his own vomit. As his body accepted death, his bowels loosened, the stench of his shit joining the stench of vomit. The merc had smelled it all before, the reeking presence of death.

"Fuck!"

"What are we going to tell Trentworth?"

"We're going to tell him fuck all. We're not supposed to be here remember? The less he knows the better."

"Now what?"

"Get some water from the Water of Leith, quickly. Use the med kit to get some of it in his lungs. Shower the body and wash it with soap, along with his clothes. Everyone wears gloves and hats. Then dump the body in the river after dark. Then we'll get the fuck out of here."

A man walking his dog along the Water of Leith path discovered the body early the next morning. It took the police over a day to figure out who it was, and only then when a senior police officer recognised the tattoo of his former regiment. The officer had spent five years in the SAS before getting injured and taken off active duty.

The initial working theory was that the Real SLA was behind the killing to avenge the killing of Jimmy McLeod. But that didn't square with the former SAS operator. He didn't think they'd want him dead, but if they did, they'd do it more dramatically, make a real show if it, an example. He would need to look into this a bit further.

Lieutenant Wilson came into Trentworth's office just after lunch with the news.

"Sir, the Edinburgh & Lothian police found a body yesterday that they have now identified as that of Sergeant Sabjirt Singh."

"What? Where? How did he die?"

"They found his body floating in the Water of Leith sir. The early report confirms the cause of death as drowning. The water in is lungs matched that from the river sir. There were no drugs or alcohol in his system".

"Thank you lieutenant, that will be all. Please keep me informed when the full report becomes available."

The lieutenant saluted smartly before he left.

Trentworth picked up his secure phone and dialled a memorised number. The phone was answered, but only silence greeted him.

"Do you know anything about this Singhe business?"

"No sir, nothing."

"Bullshit. I can hear it in your voice. You fuck wits accidentally killed him didn't you? Why didn't you tell me you had him?"

"We have our orders sir."

Trentworth knew what he meant, he'd ordered them not to tell him anything that he didn't need to know, just to sort out Fin and Birt, one way or another.

"You did the right thing. Stand down, I might need you ready if McColl shows his face again."

"Roger that."

"Well?"

"There is something not quite right. There is definitely river water in his lungs, but as you insisted, I looked at it very closely.

I think it's actually a mix of Edinburgh tap water and Water of Leith water."

"Hmmm … anything else?"

"Well, they're faint Chief Inspector, but on closer inspection I found bruises on his wrists, chest and ankles, like he'd been strapped down and struggled against the straps. And one more thing, he had bruises and cuts from his teeth on the inside of his lips."

That was it then, he knew it was murder. Scratch that, accidental murder. They'd water boarded him and it had gone wrong.

"In your professional capacity Doc, what do you think happened to him?"

"In my official capacity I can only give you the facts Chief Inspector, but if I had to speculate, I would say this man was strapped to a board and someone used some sort of device to force water into his mouth and thereby his lungs. I would say it was tap water, which after he died, was supplemented with river water."

"To cover the murder in some way?"

"Probably, or at least … forgive me sir … to cloud the waters."

Indeed, now he had to decide who to tell. First he'd better make sure the information didn't just disappear, just in case. Things had gotten a bit strange since the military had moved in.

"Can you write this up as an official report, including your speculations?"

"Carefully caveated, yes."

"Thank you. I don't need to tell you how urgent this is?"

"No you don't."

The report arrived on his desk an hour later. He made thirty copies and then called in his lieutenants.

"Right, here's what we've got on the Singhe case," he said and started to pass out the report.

"Chief Inspector do you want me to get the army liaison officer? She said she wanted to be included in any briefing on the Singhe case." A few people sniggered. It was well known that the inspector who'd spoken wouldn't mind any sort of liaison with the officer in question. Not that any of them would turn her down if the opportunity arose. Maybe it was the uniform.

"I will brief the ice queen lieutenant, let's keep this here for now shall we? He's one of ours."

The lieutenant got the message. They were sticking to form, but not exactly going out of their way to cooperate with the army.

"Singhe was murdered, probably by drowning. It looks like someone water boarded him and screwed it up. They didn't want to ask him how he knew about water boarding. It was well known he'd been in the Special Forces before coming to the police.

"So someone in the Real SLA, ex-Special Forces then?"

"Maybe, but why would they water board him? You only do that if you need information. What information would they need? Do they want Fin McColl? Would they want to hurt him when he's a national hero? No, I don't think so."

"Georgie, tell us about the incident in East Lothian."

"Right, I got a call from a patrol officer who was looking into reported helicopter noise and shouting at a farm out by Tranent. When I got to the farm there was no one there. The back door had been bashed in and there were imprints where I thought helicopters had landed. Nobody knew anything or where the elderly couple that lived there had gone. They are decent people, but everyone I spoke to knew they were in the Scottish

Independence Party. They used to pass out leaflets and canvass during elections and stuff."

"Anything else?"

"There were muddy boot marks in the house, but that isn't too abnormal for a farm house. It seemed to me that someone had slept in the loft guest room, but the bed was made and I didn't find anything strange, except . . . "

"Get on with it would you!"

"This." He held up a piece of black material.

"What about it?"

"It's a head covering, like the kind that athletic Sikhs wear, like you know, that cricket player. Look." He put it on. It looked just like the one that Birt had been wearing in photos publicised by the military police.

"Forensics turn up anything?"

"They found some body hair in the bed, I'm having it analysed now."

"I bet you anything it will be Singhe's."

"I wouldn't bet against you."

"Gentlemen, keep copies of this report on your person. I think the army or some intelligence unit had something to do with this. They could try to make that information disappear. It's our duty as Scottish citizens to not let that happen. Anyone have any issue with that or want to step away from this, say so now because this could get a bit messy."

No one moved.

"Off you go then. I'm going to see the Super. And Lieutenant, you should go brief the liaison officer," the Chief Inspector said with a grin.

"How many people have you told about your pet theories Chief Inspector?" The liaison officer's icy stare and frosty tone told him he'd been right to take precautions. He couldn't help but smirk when she talked, in spite of himself. She sounded like a recording of the Queen from thirty years ago.

"Hmmm … Well, let's see. There's the pathologist, his assistant on the post-mortem and lab tests, plus his PA who typed up the report. I also briefed my inspectors and their teams, plus the team's support officers. Oh, and then there was the Super and his number two."

"Why didn't you just issue a press release while you were at it?"

"Major, I'm just doing my job by the book, I briefed you as soon as you became available. Where have you been by the way?"

"Not that it's any of your concern Chief Inspector, but I was with the Interim Governor."

"Ah."

"I will need all copies of the lab report and anything written that includes your groundless speculation that members of British Special Forces were involved in the death of Sergeant Sabjirt Singhe."

"Of course, I have everything for you on my desk."

"Every copy?"

"I can't be sure of that Major." True enough!

"Then you'd better make sure of it Chief Inspector or I will have you charged."

"I will ask around Major."

Five minutes after the Major left, no doubt heading back over to report to Trentworth, the Chief Inspector headed to find his favourite chubby reporter, a copy of the lab report tucked into his coat.

Andy Skeen

Highland Jedi

Edinburgh, Scotland, present day

Callum Skinner had so far been left out of operations by the RSLA leadership, held in reserve. His skills lay elsewhere. They sounded desperate now that Jimmy was dead, but there were other people they could use, former service men like Callum, who specialised in psychological warfare. A mis-named activity if ever there was one. All he did was talk to people, give them ideas.

But today wasn't about talking, at least not yet. He was at a planning meeting for a protest, one that the protest leaders were adamant must be peaceful. A small fervent group of organisers were standing at the front, giving orders.

"Please keep things under control, do not antagonise the police, they're Scots, they're on our side. Don't give the army any reason to retaliate, they will be armed, this isn't like a normal protest.

"All we want is to get our message across and get press exposure. It's sheer weight of numbers we want to be seen on the telly."

Then they grew quiet.

"If anyone has … contacts, please ask them to stop what they're doing. Ask them to stay away from this protest, we don't want any trouble and we don't want anyone to get hurt. Please."

Right, Callum thought, no one to get hurt. He smiled his likeable smile and nodded. The protest had been banned, the police would try to 'kettle' the group and things would get ugly, no doubt about it.

In order to defeat the army cordons, people were planning to arrive by bike and walk, not drawing attention to themselves. Somehow the army had shut down the mobile network so the organisers bought cheap two-way radios to get organised. They knew they'd be monitored so they had a simple code.

It worked like a charm. Before the authorities had any inkling, over 5,000 people had managed to congregate into a mob that seemed to appear from nowhere. They pressed into Princes Street, stopping traffic and chanting. They unfurled banners from their rucksacks and pulled out their loudspeakers and the march was on. They screamed and yelled, demanding that the soldiers go home, that the referendum be recognised, that Scotland be free once again. Many of the banners and posters mentioned Fin, Birt and William Wallace together, calling for his immediate pardon. Many of the protestors were dressed in kilts and had painted their faces blue.

McDougal's story had worked perfectly.

The military and police scrambled to get resources in place to contain the march as it surged eastwards up Princes Street.

Callum kept near the front, the leaders trusted him, they knew him. He was 'nice'.

Tanks, actual tanks, appeared on the far end of Princes Street and soldiers poured off trucks. Police brought in from

England by the army began to close in behind, not threatening, just walking, gathering. They had prepared for something like this, rehearsed it and had a plan. A simple kettle procedure to contain the protest and let it burn itself out before it did any harm.

The army had quickly and effectively blockaded the east end of the street with barriers and further barriers were going up on side streets. The fences along the south side of the street had previously been reinforced with crowd barriers. They knew this would be the centre of any protests that erupted.

Callum moved to the front so he could get a good view, his face now showing tension, not his 'normal' friendly smiling visage. The police had closed in behind and beside, bottling the march into Princes Street.

At the barricades thrown up by the army, things had begun to get heated, with yelling and pushing. Callum joined in, waiting for the right time, searching for the cameras, waiting for them to get into good positions. He saw them and smiled. The camera people and reporters had brought out their war gear, helmets, flak jackets and safety glasses. Who knows, it might even save their lives if they got too close.

Then it started. Over the din of shouting and the occasional flying bottle or wooden protest sign, someone had begun singing the Flower of Scotland. In a flash, like at a Scotland-England football match the entire crowd joined in, replacing Edward, meaning King Edward Longshanks, William Wallace's nemesis, with the name of the current English Prime Minister...

> *O flower of Scotland*
> *When will we see*
> *Your like again*
> *That fought and died for*
> *Your wee bit hill and glen*
> *And stood against him*

Proud GORDON'S army
And sent him homeward
Tae think again

Some were evening singing in Gaelic.

O Fhlu\ir na h-Albann,
cuin a chi\ sinn
an seo\rsa laoich
a sheas gu ba\s 'son
am bileag feo\ir is fraoich,
a sheas an aghaidh
feachd uailleil Iomhair
's a ruaig e dhachaidh
air chaochladh smaoin?

Callum pushed right up a few rows of people back from the barriers and slipped his hand into the messenger bag he was carrying. He positioned the object in the bag so he could squeeze it between his left arm and body, then pulled the tab with his right hand. He pulled it quickly from the bag and heaved it over the barriers into the mass of armed British infantry beyond and ducked behind the people in front of him.

The small pipe bomb exploded almost immediately. Yes, it would injure and probably killed a few soldiers, but it was really built to make a big noise, lots of light and then smoke up the place. If he'd wanted to do real damage he'd have brought a bigger bomb, but that wasn't the point.

The screaming began and the crowd surged away from the explosion, then it happened. A soldier shot a protester who was trying to climb the barriers and suddenly several opened up on the crowd. Callum knew even bodies would not protect him from he full metal-jacketed 5.56 NATO rounds at that range so he just dropped to the ground and hoped for the best.

The screaming and firing was deafening and he was getting trampled so he scrambled to his feet just as the officers had begun to get the firing under control. But already tens of bodies lay dead or dying near the barriers.

As the firing stopped an eerie quiet fell over the massacre site, with only the sounds of weeping and the screams of the dying. The unwounded just stood aghast, trying to absorb what had just happened.

Smarting from his near trampling, he surveyed the scene. Not enough, not nearly enough. For Scotland, he would have to do more. They needed more martyrs and more blood.

The soldiers and MPs poured into the cordon with batons and begun to arrest people, all armed, full force strong-arm tactics, dragging people off, searching them, screaming at everyone to stand still or they would be shot.

They would get to him soon and he thought about dropping his bag and moving away, then thought better of it. Not nearly enough.

He slipped his hand inside the bag again, gripped the second pipe bomb under his elbow and pulled the tab. Jerking it from the bag, he pivoted towards the barricade again and threw his second bomb. The bomb arched over the barricades, toppling end over end, exploding in midair raining fragments of metal into the soldiers and medics.

At the sound of the shot, several soldiers opened fire and chaos descended once again.

McAdam put his face in his hands, his worst nightmare come to life. Deaths on both sides. There might be no way back from this, it could mean Northern Ireland all over again, maybe for years or decades. They had to let him speak, to appeal for calm and to disavow this violence. And Fin needed to get in touch, needed to distance himself from this.

The television cut away from Princes Street again.

"We're breaking away from our normal coverage for some breaking news. Major news sources in the UK have received a video by email purporting to be from the so-called Real Scottish Liberation Army. We're going to play that video now.

The screen showed a poor quality video, obviously shot by a mobile phone. It showed a single figure, a man, his face and head wrapped in a Scottish Lion Rampant flag. He carried a British Army infantry issue assault rifle. He spoke directly to the camera in a working class Glaswegian drawl.

> *"Today's actions show that we are now at war with England. We regret the loss of the innocent Scottish lives taken by the English invasion force and we will retaliate. England, you have exactly one week from today tae recognise Scotland's independence. If you dinnae, today's action was just the start. We will take the war to you, the way you have taken it to us. London, Manchester, Newcastle, Birmingham. You'll not be safe anywhere, ever again, night or day. We're everywhere and you'll never find us or catch us all. Next Monday by noon or the days of rage will dawn."*

McAdam sat dumbfounded, unable to speak. His guilt overwhelmed him. This was all his fault, his actions had put this in motion and now Scotland would no doubt pay the price. Now there was a ticking clock, only a week. He could only imagine that Gordon would dig his heels in even deeper. The man seemed to have gone mad.

Scottish Highlands, present day

Four men in suits sat and drank cokes in a corner booth, talking quietly among themselves, as they had for three straight afternoons. Oona didn't know where they were staying, maybe they were driving up each day from Fort William. They'd made no effort to hide their identity or be discrete, nor did they say anything or ask any questions. She decided they were just making the pub—and her—unavailable to Fin should he come back this way. Or maybe they were trying to send a message to him or something.

When night fell and other drinkers began trickling into the pub, they settled with a smile and disappeared from wherever they'd appeared.

Later that same night after she'd turfed out the last of the drunkards with Stevie's help—he'd always fancied her and he'd started hanging around the pub a lot lately—she headed back into the office to check his email. She hoped against hope that Fin would be able to get her a message, or something … anything.

"How you keeping lassie?"

She jumped out of her skin and shrieked at the fright.

There he stood in the kitchen. Big as life, staring at her with that dumb lovable smile on his face.

She flew into his arms bursting into tears. He held her strongly and gently, like he always had, but she felt him wince.

"What's the matter, are you hurt?"

"Bruised a bit, and the shoulder is still …"

"C'mon, let me see. Now." Her voice brooked no disagreement and they headed off to her room.

He slipped his shirt off and her eyes took in his various bruises and gashes, but the big heavy shoulder bandage dominated, showing that he was still seeping blood.

She peeled it back and gasped. He'd torn it in places and thick red blood oozed from the torn flesh.

"Let's get it cleaned up then."

The first traces of the coming dawn had just begun to lighten the sky. Fin lay in Oona's bed, watching her sleep. Their lovemaking mixed violent desperation with tenderness as their need overcame his pain.

He longed to stay, take up deerstalking on the estate again and help Oona with the pub. He would some day. He hoped.

A tap on the window broke the spell. He leapt from the bed, his hand instinctively finding the handle of the 9mm beside the bed.

He edged to the window and peered carefully through a slit in the blind without disturbing it. There stood Stevie in full deerstalking kit. He could just make out his face.

He pulled the blind open and signalled to come to the back door.

Stevie was anxious and panting, "Mate, get the fuck out of here, they're coming. I saw a convoy coming down the glen from Ben Stor. You haven't got long."

Behind him he heard Oona, "Fin? What is it?"

"I've got to go. They know I'm here, I need to get away." He began moving, quickly and purposefully. He dressed quickly, he hadn't unpacked.

"I'm sorry about this Oona... I... I love you."

She grabbed him and held him close, then stepped away. "Come back. I'll wait for you." She even managed a smile.

"I don't know what's to happen, I might end up in prison. I would understand if you didn't. I don't want you to see me as a prisoner."

"Just shut up and get out of here."

He jumped into the car and peeled away, heading east, toward the moor—his only chance. He saw the headlights in the distance as he turned onto the main road, he kept his headlights out, driving half on memory and half on instinct, wondering when the helicopter would show up.

He flicked open one of the pre-pay phones he'd been given and dialled the number he knew by heart.

"Aye?"

Fin put on his happiest voice and thickest accent.

"Hey mate, I haven't got long, the fuckin' phone is about to die. I'm headed deerstalking up tae the Col where we gave the loser the good news last time, remember? Should be there by evening if ya fancy it, bring some ponies eh? Gotta go mate!" Click.

Stevie grinned, Fin was still free! He'd better go fetch the bastard.

Rannock Moor, one of the most inhospitable, dangerous and trackless wildernesses in Britain. Mile after mile of unbroken sucking peat bog, meandering steams and heather, punctuated by the white bleached bones of the majestic old forest that once stood there.

Fin wasn't exactly prepared for this and he knew his wound was already bleeding again. In a word, he was fucked.

The first thing he did was get his pack out and then rolled the car into a deep pool of water. The cold black peaty water would keep it concealed from thermal and visual detection.

He had a gillie suit, but his heat signature was his biggest problem. The bogs would help him with that. He had another problem with heat too, keeping it in his body. He could easily die of exposure if he got wet. To survive he would need to cover over 50 miles to the southwest over boggy country, undetected.

He was definitely fucked.

"Where is he? Tell us and we'll let you go. Keep silent and you'll go to jail."

"I told you, I don't know."

"We know he was here, you're his girlfriend right? You expect me to believe that he didn't tell you where he was going?"

Oona, used to dealing with men of all types in the pub had this one figured out pretty quickly. He was mean, really mean. He would hurt her, she felt it. "I'm not lying. He was here, but he didn't tell me where he was going so that I wouldn't have to lie. I do not know."

"Then I'm detaining you under the auspices of the Terrorism Act. Let's see if some time in a cell improves your memory. Corporal!

A burly young corporal stomped into the lounge at the shout, "Sir?!"

"Arrest this woman, then send a squad over to arrest Mrs. McColl. I want them both where I can keep an eye on them. Everyone meets back at the pub car park. And keep your fucking eyes peeled, this bastard is still out there and might try something if he sees us take his woman and mother."

"Sir, right away sir."

"Oh, and send in your staff sergeant."

The corporal saluted and left smartly. The sergeant must have been listening because he marched in straightaway.

"Sir?"

"Contact Edinburgh, tell them we've got McColl trapped up here, but we're going to need men and helicopters. Have them strengthen the roadblocks and checkpoints… not that roads mean much up here."

"Yes sir."

Fin scanned 360 degrees and saw nothing. Nothing in the sky either. He'd made about ten miles so far in broad daylight, but expected that he'd have company soon. Right on time, he caught the glint of an aircraft. He eased behind a bank to have a look.

Military helicopter, quartering the moor, working from south to north. Soon another joined it. He set off, tracking a meandering root south, towards the distant choppers, keeping low and moving slow, stopping to check 360 about every hundred yards.

"Where do we think he is?"

"We've got everything covered, with lookouts and roadblocks everywhere. The only place he could be is out on Rannock Moor.

"There is absolutely no point in going into that moor. If he's in there, the only way to find him is by air. There's no buildings, nothing. I'll task in some more helicopters."

"Roger that sir."

Several hours later, tired, hungry, wet and bedraggled, Fin crawled up a gurgling burn, immersing himself in water twice on the way when helicopters eased over, quartering the ground, their infrared radar systems swivelling around. He knew he was in bad shape because he couldn't stop shivering. He'd need to get out of the water soon if he wasn't going to die of hypothermia.

The choppers had panicked a herd of female red deer at one point, which nearly trampled him as he lay invisible in his ghillie suit, half covered in freezing water.

He wasn't too cold to reflect on the idea that training aside, this was probably the first time a ghillie suit had been used for its original purpose in the Highlands where it had been invented, hiding from other men, since Victorian times. Estate gamekeepers had invented them to hide from and catch deer poachers on Highland sporting estates. Those same men had been the ones who had invented sniping and kept its traditions alive from the Boer War and the Crimea, to the African campaigns in WWI.

There were hundreds of deer around, which no doubt helped confuse matters. Still, they found Stevie without any issue and one of the choppers buzzed him, scattering his Highland ponies. It sat down nearby and a squad of soldiers poured out, forming a perimeter and surrounding Stevie, who stood there with his hands up.

Fin pulled himself out of the burn just a few hundred yards away, hidden in tall heather, shaking uncontrollably with cold. The chopper would hide any noise and the wind would conceal any movement he made. He rubbed himself and rolled about trying to get warm, before rolling to his stomach and crawling up where he could get a view of Stevie.

His friend had understood his message perfectly and come to the col where Birt had shot the old stag who'd lost his last fight several weeks before. He'd brought his three deer ponies too, including Shitehead, but they had scattered, no doubt well on their way back to their stables by now.

Stevie had his hands up with three soldiers in full combat gear surrounding him, one searched him while the others covered him with rifles. Another held his deerstalking rifle. Fin watched as an officer got off the chopper and walked over.

After much gesturing and pointing down in the valley the officer seemed satisfied. Stevie didn't look anything like Fin and had just enough gut on him—a legacy of spending too much time at The Poacher's Pint—to convince anyone that he was no Special Forces soldier. He gave an order and the squad headed back to the chopper.

Fin rolled back into the burn as the chopper took off and roared overhead. He waited until it topped the ridge and disappeared before rolling back out shaking and shivering again. He rolled onto his back and searched the sky carefully for any other choppers. He could hear Stevie whistling for his ponies as he came down the mountain towards him.

He waited until his mate got within about 20 feet before jumping to his feet.

"Shit!" He fell flat on his arse, trying to scramble backwards up the hill like a crab on his hands and feet before recovering himself. "Fin?!"

Laughing despite himself, "Yeah mate, it's me!"

"Jesus, Mary and Father, are you trying to fucking kill me! You're a bastard ya know that!"

"Yeah."

"All right then?"

"Well, I could use a pint mate, or maybe a cuppa?"

Stevie laughed in delight at finding his friend alive and well, once he recovered from the shock of having a green heather monster appear out of the ground. He pulled a flask of hot tea out of his rucksack and poured a shot of it into the lid/cup. "I made tea, I've got a hip flask of the good stuff too."

"Tea first," Fin took it, hands shaking. It was steeped to the point of sharp bitterness cut by enough sugar in it to rot the teeth of three men. It also burned his lip and mouth, but he didn't care, it was the best cup of tea he'd ever had.

"What now Fin? Do you have a plan?"

"Aye mate, first we need to find your ponies."

"They'll be around, they won't go far and will come to the whistle."

"Good stuff Stevie, you always were better with the ponies than me. Let's find them, then let's go deerstalking."

"Why the hell for?"

"You'll see!"

The hike up the ridge warmed Fin right back up. He crawled forward, easing himself through the heather, still in his sniper suit. He knew where the deer would be, they felt safe this high, even when they'd been spooked and stampeded by multiple helicopter 'sorties'. He got the feeling the pilots were enjoying scattering the deer.

And there they all were, over a hundred hinds—female red deer—and yearlings, right where he expected them to be. But they were panicky and alert as a result of all the activity and helicopters. He'd taken Stevie's stalking rifle and left him farther down the hill with the ponies. He'd had to circle over a mile out of his way to stay downwind and out of sight of the nervous herd.

He'd made it to under 200 yards and wasn't going to get any closer without sending the entire herd over the top of the ridge and out of sight. He inspected the herd, looking for an old yeld, a female without any young. After fifteen minutes of carefully searching through the herd, he found her. She was big too, maybe big enough for the job he had in mind for her.

Fin always found something very sad about yelds. The rest of the female deer in a herd seemed to turn bitchy about them. They found themselves getting bitten and kicked by females with young. Sometimes yelds were completely driven out of a herd by its animosity. This one seemed to only suffer the occasional nip or kick whenever it was convenient for the milling females. It meant she was also on the outside of the herd and sometimes chased away from any youngsters she might accidentally get close to. Maybe that was it, they were afraid she'd try to steal their fawns.

He waited several minutes until the yeld, sides heaving from being chased about, stood apart from the bunch. She was limping badly too. That settled it. He didn't want to kill anymore. He thought he was done with that, but he needed a deer and this one was injured, so he could put it out of its misery.

He settled the crosshairs of Stevie's fancy, eye-wateringly expensive German-made riflescope, a gift from a German client, on the yeld's vitals. He knew the rifle could easily equal any sniper rifle in accuracy because Stevie had spent so much time fiddling with it. He'd put on a match barrel and carefully mated the action to the stock with fibreglass bedding compound to ensure accuracy. He'd also installed a target match trigger and set it to break at just over one pound of force, or what someone who knew nothing about shooting would call a 'hair trigger.' It made sense to have the best tools to do the job and Stevie had spent his life managing this deer herd, taking Fin's place when he'd run off to join the army.

The yeld turned broadside presenting a perfect target, with no other deer around her or behind her that might get hit accidentally. The American-made match trigger broke from its seer crisply, releasing the firing spring to slam into the primer of the cartridge.

All working deerstalking rifles these days are mounted with sound moderators to protect estate and forestry workers from damaging their hearing over a lifetime of managing deer herds. So instead of the muzzle blast and heavy recoil of a military sniper rifle, the moderator soaked up much of the blast and some of the sound as the .308 inch diameter projectile exited the barrel.

He'd made a perfect shot, severing the yeld's spinal column. She dropped on the spot like a sack of shit, dead before she hit the ground. The herd of hinds milled about trying to figure out where the threat was coming from before heading over the ridge and away.

By the time Stevie arrived with the ponies, Fin had the gralloch out of the deer, pulling it away.

"What now Fin?"

"Do you remember when Luke Skytrooper crawled inside that big fuck off kangaroo thing to hide from the stormwalkers, or whatever the fuck they were?"

Stevie suddenly got why they needed a deer and started laughing. He walked over to the where the yeld lay to inspect Fin's work with a practiced practical eye. He'd not done a standard gralloching job. Instead of the traditional cut from sternum to pelvis, he'd made a single cut above her dry milk sack to the inside of each thigh, crossways to the traditional cut. He'd pulled out the guts and organs through this hole.

"You're going to crawl inside her? Man, there is no way you're going to fit."

"I'll fit, mostly. We'll just have to cover what doesn't with the canvas tarpaulin."

Stevie thought it might just work. The tough sturdy garron ponies could certainly manage the weight of the deer and Fin together, they'd carried much bigger stags before. Now they just had to get the deer on the pony and Fin in the deer.

It took a lot of cussing and coaxing of the skittish pony, which wasn't at all sure about whatever it was they were doing on his back, but eventually, Fin had jammed himself fully inside the big yeld, only his head and shoulders poking out nestled neatly between her thighs.

Stevie couldn't help but chuckle at the sight of him.

"Fuck you Stevie, just take me home."

"Your mum's gone mate, the MPs took her."

"They leave anyone behind to watch the place?"

"Probably. They took Oona too."

"Yeah." Fin felt a sharp pang of guilt at the confirmation that they'd arrested Oona after his escape.

"Best take you to my place, I can get you out of there in the stables out of sight."

Stevie secured the deer firmly to the pony, with Fin inside, covering both with a canvas tarpaulin, but leaving the head clearly visible to any observer.

"You all right, can you breathe?"

"It smells, I'm going to cramp up in this position and I'm covered in blood, but I'll live. Just get me the fuck home."

On the way down, they were buzzed twice by helicopters that came back around to investigate, but none landed. Fin had a dicey moment when the garron he was on tried to buck the deer off and flee the terrifying helicopter, but Stevie had done a good job securing the deer and he managed to calm the terrified pony.

Stevie had heaved a deep sigh of relief when he turned into the stable yard off the pony trail, thinking he was home free, when an Army Land Rover Defender turned into the yard.

An older soldier, not in combat gear, stepped from the vehicle and Stevie realised with a jolt that he knew the man. He was one of the estate owner's friends and Stevie had taken him deerstalking a few times.

"Good day Steven, out deerstalking eh?"

"Yes sir, I was culling today when all this hell broke loose."

"Say, isn't that a hind? Aren't they out of season?"

"Yes sir, it's a yeld. She had a bad leg so I put her out of her misery." Stevie just hoped he didn't want to inspect the deer's leg.

"She's big isn't she?"

"Yes sir," time for a distraction, "Are you staying nearby sir? I could bring you around some liver for your breakfast, I remember that you like it."

"No thank you Steven, I'll head back to Fort William shortly. You haven't seen Finlay have you? I know you're his friend."

"No sir, not since Thursday when he came to the pub, I saw him then, but not since." Better to give him something, he wouldn't be as suspicious.

"So you did see him Thursday?"

"Yes sir, he was here. Came to the pub."

"Yes, he did. We know about that. Well, if you see him … well, I don't expect you'll call me, but maybe you'd tell him he'd be better off if he surrendered. I'd hate to have to tell his mother he was dead."

"If I see him, I'll tell him what you said sir."

"Thank you Steven, enjoy that liver for me won't you? Good bye."

Fin had nearly passed out from lack of air when Stevie pulled him heaving and sputtering from between the yeld's legs. Stevie couldn't help but laugh at the absurdity of it, "That's the most action you're going to get for awhile mate."

He immediately regretted saying it when he saw the brooding look that settled onto Fin's face. The comment had inadvertently reminded him that Oona had been arrested and that the chances were that if he survived this ordeal, they'd only see each other behind the glass on visitor's day. If they let him have visitors.

Stevie snuck Fin into his house after dark, only after he agreed to strip off all his bloody clothes. After a long hot shower, Stevie fed him on deer liver, fried with onions and a big helping of neeps and tatties—parsnips and potatoes. Fin usually had no trouble eating whatever anyone put in front of him, but his performance impressed even Stevie, who was used to seeing Fin polish off his own weight in food since they were boys.

With deep glasses of Glen Livet in hand, they settled down to watch a bit of the news and talk about how they were going to get Fin out of the Highlands.

Birt's face greeted them as soon as they turned on the television.

> *"In case you're just joining us, police authorities have confirmed the identity of the body of the Asian man found in Edinburgh's Water of Leith yesterday morning as that of fugitive Special Forces soldier Sergeant Sabjirt Singhe of Glasgow."*

Fin stood up.

*"In a further dramatic development, a newspaper
reporter received an evidence file from an anonymous
source that seemed to suggest that Sergeant Singhe had
been restrained and drowned, perhaps by some form of
water boarding.*

*"A spokesperson from the Scotland Military Authority
now in charge of all of Scotland under Martial Law, said
that any suggestion of involvement by the British Military
or British intelligence operatives in the death of Sergeant
Singhe was absurd. He went on to suggest that breakaway
factions of the Scottish Liberation Army were responsible
for Singhe's death."*

Fin didn't notice as the glass of whisky slipped from his
hand.

"Trentworth. That cunt he did this. I can't believe Birt's
dead."

"How do you know?"

Fin sat back down, "We … I … think he's using
mercenaries. He was cuddly with them back in Afghan, the
Americans assigned him a close protection detail. Who else? SAS
wouldn't harm one of their own and the spooks don't have the
balls to water board anyone. They'd just stand by and collect the
intel."

"Calm down man, think about this." The look on Fin's face
scared Stevie. He'd never seen Fin like this, at once angry and
sad.

"I promise you Stevie, that fucker is dead, I'm going to kill
him with my own hands. I should have just let Jimmy fucking do
it." He couldn't escape from the guilt he felt over Birt's death,

added to the death of the security forces that Jimmy had killed. Everything was going to shit.

He sat back down and Stevie retrieved his glass, refilled it and handed it back.

Fin was used to death and losing comrades in combat, but Birt was different. They'd worked together for over ten years, for so long they didn't need to speak most of the time. Birt made a show of tagging along because he was a Scot too. That may have been part of it, but Fin suspected he came out of loyalty to him. Birt's death needed to mean something and Trentworth needed to pay. He thought about tracking down and killing the mercenaries, he could probably do it. Maybe he would later, but for now, Trentworth.

Less than twenty minutes later, he was driving out of Dunfeldy in an MP's Land Rover, siren screaming as he headed East, the former occupants of the front seat now fast asleep in the back. They just waved him through the checkpoint.

Andy Skeen

Shopping day

BBC News
"The government has issued a statement this evening confirming that there would be no change in policy towards Scotland, and denying any knowledge of the events that led up to the death of Sergeant Sabjirt Singhe, blaming factions of the Scottish Liberation Army.

"The statement promised a full investigation to ensure that no element of the military or government had any involvement in Singhe's death.

"The search for Finlay McColl continues at this hour, with rumours that he has been cornered in his home village of Dunfeldy in the Scottish Highlands. Reporters are being kept out of the area and it appears to be under a complete lock down.

"A military spokesman confirmed that McColl's mother, one Elisabeth McColl, and a known associate, thought to be his girlfriend Oona MacLean, had both been detained under the Terrorism Act."

No. 10 Downing Street, London, England, present day

"Edward, what do you know about this?"

Silence.

"You told me to get it done," Trentworth finally said.

"You killed this soldier?"

"Michael, it was an accident".

"Were British soldiers involved in, or witness to, this man's death?"

"None. No serving British Forces personnel were involved, there is no paper trail. They were using any and all means necessary to locate and apprehend Staff Sergeant Finlay McColl, as per my orders. We thought he was the killer then. I'm still not convinced that he isn't and that he pulled the wool over that reporter's eyes."

"If this is traced back to you I won't be able to protect you Edward, I won't be able to protect myself."

"I'll sort this out Michael, don't worry."

"Zoë! Get in here!" the Prime Minister yelled.

She jumped at the harshness of the PM's voice. She'd only ever heard that tone in the bedroom. He liked it a little rough.

She popped her head in, "Prime Minister?"

"I need to issue a statement to the press about this Sabjirt Singhe business ... and the future of Scotland."

There was no way he was giving this up. This office, his women, his power. What stupidity this all was—ignorant, nationalist, brutal, animalistic stupidity! He wasn't going to give in, not one fucking inch. He wasn't going to end up in prison over this Singhe business either, he would let Edward go down for that one. He would draft the press statement, then make some calls. Best convene COBRA too, to make it all seem legit. They would back him though, none of them wanted to be the ones that broke up the Union ... and lose their power at the same time.

Rural Kent, Southern England, present day

Fin gripped the steering wheel of a 'borrowed' Japanese 4x4 pickup truck, as he drove into England along logging roads in Keilder Forest wearing night vision goggles. He had a plan, he needed to draw Trentworth out so he could put a bullet in his head.

He didn't know why he did it, but he stopped at an Internet café in a non-descript market town along the back way to London. The drive took him most of a day since he avoided the main routes and instead, took a meandering country lane route using his mum's satnav that a friend had got her for Christmas.

At the Internet café it took him about twenty minutes to find the address he was looking for. They'd been trained in the CRW how to find people on the Internet in a pinch, and, surprisingly, the unit logon credentials all still worked.

Several hours and hundreds of miles later, he cruised past a moderately sized country residence in rural Kent. Still not sure what he was going to do, feeling jittery and uncharacteristically indecisive, he checked for security and found none. No cameras, no guards, nothing.

He came back around and pulled into the drive, stopping at the front door. His hand searched into the bergen he had on the passenger seat and found his issue 9mm sidearm, withdrew it from its holster and tucked it into his jeans behind his back. When he stood up, he straightened his jacket so that it covered it completely, then strode to the door and pressed the bell. He still had no idea what he was doing here, or what he planned to say.

A small, frail, sad-looking woman opened the door to him without checking the peephole, "Yes? Can I help you?"

"Mrs. Trentworth?"

"Yes, I'm Imogen Trentworth."

"Mrs. Trentworth, I'm a ... friend of your husband's. Do you recognise me? Is the General in?"

She looked at him a long time, then said, "No and no, but you're from the Army aren't you? Lots of Edward's friends from the services stop by to see him so it's hard to remember them all," she gave him a kindly sad smile.

She was used to army officers dropping by, she just assumed this carefully groomed and well-dressed young man with bleached blond hair was one of those. He must be retired, she thought, since he also had a neatly trimmed blond goatee beard.

"I'm sorry Edward isn't home, but I was about to have an after dinner cup of tea. Could I offer you one?" She was happy for the company, to be honest. She hated the television and Edward had been gone such a long time. She was getting a bit lonely lately.

"Yes ma'am, I could surely use one."

She ushered him into the front sitting room, then disappeared to make the tea. The room gave Fin an immediate and clear understanding of the Trentworths. They were as upper class as you can get, but without old money left. The house itself was relatively new, but every piece of furniture looked antique. This was not a couple who had ever bought a piece of their own furniture, it had all been inherited. Old threadbare Arab rugs covered new wooden flooring. Even to Fin, the furniture looked out of place in what appeared to be a 1950s built country bungalow.

He moved to look at the family picture corner, looked over by an oil painting of some ancestor or other of Trentworth. He looked just like the General and was in a 19th century military dress uniform.

There were tens of pictures there, mostly of a young man that at first he thought was the General himself. With a start he realised that they were too new, too recent to be the General. He must have a son. The boy was a soldier, looked like Royal Marines. Fin wondered if he'd ever met him.

"That's James, our son. I'm sorry, I forgot to ask you your name."

"Um, My name is Burton, ma'am, Burton Singhe."

"Singhe eh? Strange, you don't look Indian."

"It's ... a complicated story, my great grandmother ... during the Raj."

"Ah, say no more."

Fin took a sip of tea, wondering what the hell to say, what he was doing here, what he was looking for.

"Thank you for the tea Mrs. Trentworth, it's delicious. Not like what we drank in the army," he said with a smile.

"You're welcome."

"Your son, he's Royal Marines?"

"Yes he was," she paused, looking very sad, "His father was very disappointed when he didn't go into the Army, but I think he wanted to ... not get any special treatment because of his father."

Fin sensed there was much more to that story than she was saying, and he hadn't missed that she'd referred to her son in the past tense.

"He's out of the commandos now?"

"No, no, he ... passed on. He was killed. They said it was a training accident. He fell off a scaffold. He was so determined, but he ... got vertigo."

"Ah. I'm sorry I asked Mrs. Trentworth."

"No, you weren't to know Mr. Singhe."

'Fucking hell, what the hell am I doing here? I need to get away from this', Fin thought. This woman didn't have anything to do with Birt's death, or his father's. She sure as shit didn't have anything to do with Scotland's freedom and he didn't want to scare her now. He took a long pull of his tea and stood up.

"Thank you for the tea Mrs. Trentworth. Please if you could tell the General that Burt Singhe stopped by to pay his respects, I would be most grateful."

Mrs. Trentworth stood with him, "Of course Mr. Singhe," she said extending her hand. She began to realise something wasn't quite right, that this young man was acting slightly strangely and she might have made a mistake letting him in so easily. He also hadn't mentioned his rank, which was very odd indeed. And that name, Burt Singhe, did sound strangely familiar, but she couldn't place it. But it looked like he was getting ready to leave, which put her mind at rest.

She extended her hand to be shaken, and the young man smiled, but it was a sad smile.

"I'll take my leave now Mrs. Trentworth," he said, hoping he didn't sound like a twat speaking so formally. It just seemed like the right thing to say, and with that, he turned and walked to the door.

London, England, present day

Fin marvelled at how many bicycles were blasting around the streets of London. It hadn't been like this the last time he'd been there, but then, that was before the Boris Bike scheme and congestion charging had come in.

He knew central London fairly well though, as a result of being assigned a few times to close protection duty for visiting foreign dignitaries who were under threat. There were also a number of anti-terrorism ops that the public knew nothing about that the SAS had assisted in.

He cruised along London's most famous shopping street, Oxford Street, on a full suspension mountain bike, set up for street riding. He also had on his full-face downhill racing helmet and a cyclists' facemask air filter he'd picked up at Evans Cycles. He didn't look at all out of place, lots of people had them.

When he reached Oxford Circus, he bunny hopped the curb and dismounted quickly before he could be told off for riding on the pavement. He took off his Bergen and pretended to be searching around in it, while he pulled the detonator. It had about fifteen minutes on it. Plenty of time.

He then fished out the pay-as-you-go phone he'd purchased minutes before with cash, using Birt's name, he was sure his mate wouldn't mind. He counted two foot patrols of police just in his line of sight and knew the CCTV cameras had every inch of this stretch of road under constant surveillance. They would be on him in seconds.

He dialled 999.

"Emergency services," the voice answered, "how can I help?"

"You can shut up and listen. This is Sabjirt Singhe. I have just left a bomb on Oxford Circus next to the phone booth on the south side of the street, check the CCTV, it's there. It's strong enough to do some real damage and I know what I'm doing. If you touch it, it will go off, so don't. Clear the street now, this is no fucking joke. Use the name Sabjirt Singhe in your computer, it will tell you what you need to know."

He clicked off the phone, jumped on his bike and began to cruise nonchalantly away from where he'd dropped his Bergen. Just seconds later he could hear police whistles, sirens and shouting in the distance behind him as the Bobbies cleared the Circus and stopped traffic. He had no problems though, he just cruised away.

Police Constable Jenny Stone took the call from emergency services and immediately alerted her superiors in the CCTV monitoring station near Oxford Street. She selected a camera and turned it into the Circus, zooming in on the phone booth. There it was, a simple camouflage army Bergen, obviously full of something.

The police had already managed to clear the streets and pavements so she had a good view of the Bergen. Her supervisor had joined her, "Put that up on the big screen." She did that with a click of her mouse.

She then selected another screen and brought up the recording from a camera, cycled through it quickly but no luck, it had been pointed down at the pavement, not at the phone booth. She ran through three more recordings without seeing anything. Her supervisor knew enough to stay silent and let her do her thing. Jenny was the best in the business, personally responsible for the identification and eventual capture of scores of pickpockets and snatch-and-grab muggers all using her ability to run the CCTV system effectively.

Then she had it. A cyclist had pulled up to the phone booth, put his bag on the ground and made a phone call. "Bloody hell, he called 999 while standing over the bomb!" his supervisor exclaimed in her ear. "Quick Jenny, make some prints of that still and put it out on the network too. He's probably long gone, but you never know."

Police had cordoned off the area around the suspect package and had started to clear the buildings, but a TV crew, alerted by a journalist named McDougal from a sister company in Scotland, had already made it to a rooftop and set up a camera pointing down the street at Oxford Circus. Minutes after Fin's call, they were live on the major networks.

Fin had kept moving for another ten minutes, then, according to plan, he ditched his bike, helmet and facemask in an alley before the CCTV crews could get their act together and find him. He pulled off his jacket, leaving a long sleeve t-shirt underneath and donned the baseball cap he'd stuffed in the pocket. He left the bike behind a rubbish bin so it couldn't be seen from the street and walked out, blending into the busy street full of shoppers. Not hurrying, but not loafing about, he walked another hundred metres and into a Tube station. Using a travel pass he'd purchased earlier, he boarded a Victoria Line train north.

"What have you got Jenny?"
"I've tracked him from Oxford Circus, let me show you." She ran through the sequence of recordings she'd pieced together of Fin cycling down Oxford Street, then turning off before disappearing down an alley.
"There's no camera coverage on the other end of the alley sir, but he didn't emerge from this end."
"Clever bugger, isn't he."

"However, I did check the cameras up and down the street on the other end of the alley and found this. Not much to go on sir." She brought up a figure of a man in jeans and a dark jacket, wearing a baseball cap that effectively hid his face. He seemed to know where all the cameras were, tilting his head just so. Still, they'd both seen enough footage of Finlay McColl to know his walk. "I think it's Finlay McColl sir."

"I think you're exactly right."

Then the large screen that dominated the monitoring room suddenly lit up in a huge yellow explosion.

> ### Sky News
> "These pictures are live from Oxford Street where we received a coded tip off from an anonymous source about a terrorist alert. Scotland Yard has confirmed that there is an anti-terrorist operation in progress around Oxford Circus. As you can see, the police have cleared the streets. The police are saying that they received a 999 call from someone with a Scottish accent claiming to be Sergeant Sabjirt Singhe informing them that a bomb had been placed on Oxford Circus. It is fair to say that this action may be in retaliation for the killing of Sabjirt Singhe, which is alleged to have been an accidental death by military security forces acting under the direction of Interim Governor of Scotland, Edward Trentworth.
>
> "The camouflage bag you can see in the pictures below apparently contains the bomb. We understand that the Bomb Squad is on the way with a bomb-diffusing robot."

At that moment, exactly twenty minutes after Fin had pulled the det, the bomb exploded.

Gregor McAdam sat drinking tea in his lounge. He'd been a bit nervous about this, wondering if McColl could pull it off.

There'd seemed like too many possible things that could go wrong, but it looked beautiful.

The 'bomb' had exploded with nothing more than a loud pop, then the built in tubular 'firework' had blown thousands of three-inch square paper bright yellow and crimson Scottish Lion Rampant flags high into the air. They blanketed most of Oxford Circus, and the approaching bomb disposal robot.

'Well done my boy, well done,' Gregor thought chuckling, while one of his minders ground his teeth behind him.

Fin too started chuckling when he watched replays of the explosion a few hours later, holed up in the flat of a South African ex-Regiment friend in Hereford. The guy acted as a clearing agent for ex-Regiment soldiers looking for work on the security circuit. He was constantly trying to get Fin to come onto the circuit and make some proper money.

He also handled logistics for some of the smaller security firms, making him a very useful friend to have because he knew everybody and every trick needed to move men and guns quietly anywhere in the world.

They chinked their whisky glasses together, "glad to see you're putting your training to good use my man."

He needed to lay low for awhile, but he had a plan for getting back to Scotland. He couldn't risk the road again, but his mate was a water junkie and had a nice sailboat. Just what he needed, a nice leisurely sail to get away from the heat. Let the English think about what it would mean to have real bombs on the street, having had their security services made to look like utter fools.

He heard his name on the telly and tuned back in to what they were saying, "Dermott, this has the look and feel of the

Dewhurst incident, which therefore has Finlay McColl's fingerprints all over it. Like the Dewhurst operation, this is designed to make the security forces look like a laughing stock, while also reminding us that we are ultimately totally vulnerable to terrorist attack of this type right here in England."

The screen started showing various pictures of him, including those supplied by the army and some taken off CCTV cameras in London

"If he'd wanted to he could have killed or injured hundreds of people, but he's shown over and over again that he doesn't want to hurt anyone, just get our attention. But we all know that there are people out there without McColl's restraint. This action really raises the stakes for the British Government. With public opinion starting to turn badly against Prime Minister Gordon, everyone is now wondering what the Prime Minister will do next."

The screen cut back to Oxford Street, still covered in little Scottish flags.

'Aye,' Fin thought, 'time to go sailing. Time to go home. Time to see Oona.'

A glorious gilded cage

BBC News

"We're going live to our EU correspondent in Brussels, Ben Sonnebourne. Ben, what's happened?"

"Gemma, the European Parliament just passed a resolution calling for the immediate recognition of Scottish independence. The resolution stopped short of recognising Scotland as a separate country, but it hinted that it might.

"This joins a UN Security Council resolution, which had softer wording, but still condemned the UK government's heavy handed approach to this crisis."

Buckingham Palace, London, England, present day

What a ridiculous position to be in, an inmate in a glorious gilded prison, with bejewelled shackles and an army of servants, guards really, attending to his every need. He was doomed to this fate from the moment the Royal Physician declared, "it's a boy!"

Ironically, most 'normal' people envied his position, begrudging him his 'privileges'. If they only knew how swiftly he would change places with any one of them if he could.

He'd loved the military. It had been reassuringly humanising to have someone shout in his face the same as any other cadet, to be punished when he screwed things up, to sleep

245

in a bunk, to get wet and cold and not have some snivelling sycophant wipe his nose for him. Unfortunately, his military career had been cut painfully short by the family curse, the chronic inability to manage romantic relationships. Or, in this particular case, an inveterate sideline interest in fetching young butlers.

He had accepted his duty without question or hesitation. His father had asked and there could be only one answer. Now he was King George the VII of England, Scotland and Northern Ireland, while his father went walking alone at Balmoral, a broken man.

He understood the word 'Duty' in a way perhaps that would have made more sense two hundred years ago, although he had encountered a similar understanding among many of his fellow officers in the military.

King George also knew that this sense of duty he'd encountered in the military is what drove Fin McColl, the so-called New William Wallace. The young king despised unnecessary violence, but the Scot had as yet only made war in military terms. He'd gone to great lengths, and put himself at grave risk, to avoid hurting any civilians. Some press reports had indicated that he'd played a hand in keeping hot-headed elements of the nationalist movements from more rash action. None of that spoke to a desire to mindlessly terrorise or destroy.

So, here he sat, the sovereign, in name at least, of two countries—one where he'd been born, the other where he'd spent his summers and been educated—on the verge of exploding in a nasty terrorist guerrilla war. Northern Ireland would look like a picnic given that many of the UK's Special Forces were in fact Scottish and had already deserted, declaring their loyalty to a free Scotland.

And he couldn't do a damned thing about it, could he? He wished his grandmother were still here. She'd know exactly what to do.

He had been taught about constitutional law by special Household tutors of course, but he'd always thought it was pretty pointless. It was a constitutional monarchy after all. Decisions were made by Prime Ministers and Parliament in the King's name, with most of the powers of the Crown being purely symbolic.

What much of the general public didn't fully appreciate, however, is that a lot of power in truth still rested with the Monarchy in the form of the Royal Prerogative. Custom and tradition alone decreed that the Monarchs exercised their powers in consultation with the Prime Minister, but ultimately neither his, nor Parliament's, approval was required for the King to exercise certain Royal Prerogatives—at least in theory.

In the present circumstances, the most important aspects of the Prerogative were those making him head of the Armed Forces. The Sovereign and Sovereign alone had the power to declare war, make peace and direct military action. Every soldier, officer and enlisted, took an oath of loyalty to the Monarch and many took that oath seriously. Each and every regiment of the British Armed Forces met separately with the Monarch, updating him on their deployment or readiness status. He had personal, direct access far down the chain of command.

He also had access to the heads of state of all recognised foreign governments and institutions, as the official the Head of State of the United Kingdom. In that capacity he held hundreds of audiences a year with ambassadors, presidents, trade delegations and representatives of supra-governmental organisations, such as the EU and UN.

Most of his subjects were blissfully unaware of real behind-the-scenes role of the Monarch and tended to think of him and of the Royal Family as an indispensable tradition, a useful tourist attraction, or a pointless drain on the public coffers, depending on their politics. Customarily the Monarch simply signed orders drawn up by the Government, although in private they had often asked hard questions. But that practice had no real legal basis, only tradition and custom. Ultimately, however, power rested with him. The Royal sceptre that graced the chamber of the House of Commons next to the Despatch Box, was there as a reminder that the House exercised power on behalf of the Monarch, not in its own right.

But, if he, or indeed any king, ever tried to exercise those powers overtly, it had been made very clear to him by his tutors and courtiers that it would set in motion a chain of political events that would probably lead to the end of the Monarchy itself.

That was his choice: act to try and save his country and potentially destroy his country's most beloved institution, or sit on his hands and save the Monarchy, while watching the country tear itself apart.

No. 10 Downing Street, London, England, present day

"Prime Minister?"

"Yes June?"

"I have the Palace on the phone sir."

That's odd, what would they want and why now, in the middle of all this?

"Sir, it's actually … well, it's the King himself sir, making a direct call.

Slightly alarmed now, "Put him through."

He picked up the phone as soon as it rang, "Your Majesty?"

"Prime Minister."

The young king sounded odd, strained even, and now he was silent.

"Is there something I can help you with Your Majesty?"

"Yes, yes there is. I would like you to come to the Palace. Today please."

"Sir, things are a little complicated just at the moment, if I could come tomorrow."

"It's rather urgent, I would think this afternoon would be for the best."

What the hell was going on here?

"Well, okay sir, I will come as soon as I can."

"Very good, I'll be waiting."

The heavily armoured Jaguar rolled smoothly through the carriage gate into the courtyard of Buckingham Palace after screaming down the Mall with a police escort. The Prime Minister was in a hurry and wanted to get this over with so he could get back to dealing with the Scottish problem.

A courtier was there, waiting to escort him to the King's audience chamber, which was empty when he arrived.

A silver tea service appeared just as he sat down to await the King. The impeccably turned-out butler carefully sugared and milked his tea just the way he liked it and retreated without saying a word.

Then a courtier opened the double doors and announced the King, forcing the PM to hurriedly set his tea down and jump to attention, feeling a bit like a naughty schoolboy. He supposed monarchs always had that effect on people, despite the man being twenty years his junior.

"Please sit, I shan't keep you long. I've come to a decision. I want you to know that I have thought long and hard about this and I want you to understand that I fully comprehend the potential ramifications of what I am about to say.

"I want you to work out a deal with Gregor McAdam that recognises Scottish independence—

"Your Majesty this—"

"Please do not interrupt!" the king slammed his hand down on the tea table, rattling the china and silver tea service.

I've made my decision. If you do not do this, I will be forced to exercise the Royal Prerogative. I have a number of options at my disposal, including giving orders directly to the army to leave Scotland, withdrawing Royal Asset for the 1707 Act of Union as passed by the English Parliament, or indeed giving Royal Asset to the Scottish Articles rescinding the Act of Union, as legally passed by the Scottish Parliament. Let's not forget that I am still officially the Head of State for both countries.

"I know what this means Prime Minister, both for myself and for the Monarchy, but your actions leave me little choice. I cannot let you continue to take these actions in my name and I feel compelled to act. The decision is yours to make now. You have one day. I expect you to report back to me tomorrow on what action you will take."

With that the King simply stood up and walked out of the room.

He was so shocked he forgot to stand when the King stood, he just sat there open mouthed for several minutes, before the butler arrived.

"Sir, can I get you anything else?"

"Yes Donald, I desperately need a drink. Scotch on the rocks please."

Perfectly trained, Donald didn't react, but inside he was smirking, both at the double layer of irony of the Prime Minister's order and at what he had just overheard. His Scottish mother would be so proud of the King if she knew!

Donald had obliged him with a second whisky before he'd departed Buckingham Palace. He'd needed time to think, so he took it. He thought he could neuter the King with a pre-emptive strike of some sort. He just needed get with his advisers and figure it out.

But what had been a very bad day, turned into the worst day of his life when he arrived back at No. 10. June was waiting for him at the door when he arrived.

"Sir, there are several unannounced visitors, I didn't know what to do so I put them in the Cabinet Room." June looked distressed.

"What? Who are they?" angry now, the Prime Minister couldn't believe June's stupidity. She was normally so reliable and always knew the appropriate etiquette,

"It's most of the Cabinet, sir, and several other people."

He gritted his teeth and stormed passed her towards the Cabinet Room. What he found there stunned him speechless. The most powerful men and women in government stood or sat in the room. They turned silent and still the second he appeared in the door.

"What is this? What's going on?" he demanded. He knew perfectly well what was going on, he just needed to stall for time, figure out what to do.

As June had said, most of the Cabinet was there, all of his Party friend/enemies. Unusually, they were attended by Permanent Secretaries, the senior civil servant in each of their Ministries. Likewise, the Leader of the Opposition, what the hell was she doing here? His eyes searched further as no one spoke, no one stepped forward to offer an explanation of their presence.

He saw with astonishment that the Speaker of the House of Commons and the Leader of the House of Lords stood together. Both were supposedly non-political appointments so he wondered what they could possibly have with a Party rebellion. Then he spotted the Metropolitan Police Commissioner standing with the Chiefs of Staff of the branches of the armed forces.

This was no Party rebellion, no palace coup, this was the end. It was over, all of it was finished.

Finally it was left to his old friend, the Party Secretary who spoke, "Sir, if you resign ... "

The PM finished the sentence for him, "I won't be arrested? Stuck in the Tower of London? Beheaded? For what? For trying to keep this country together? If I resign, what?"

"We won't have to table a resolution to remove you from office."

Yes, it was truly over. He wondered if the King had put them up to this. Probably, he thought, the timing was too convenient. He had nothing left but his dignity and he would keep that now, at all costs.

"Fine." He turned and spoke back into the open doorway where his personal secretary was standing, stricken, "June, can you ask the Press Secretary to join us? Her speechwriting skills are required."

Westminster Hall, London, England, present day

"If you have tuned in expecting to watch Eastenders, it will follow this broadcast in thirty minutes' time. We're going live to Westminster Hall where the Prime Minister is going to make an address regarding the crisis in Scotland."

The PM strode forcefully and with determination to the podium amid a crescendo of flash photography. No one spoke, there were no shouted questions.

"My Cabinet colleagues and myself, along with senior civil servants and members of His Majesty's Opposition have met this afternoon in a spirit of non-partisanship to discuss the future of the United Kingdom.

"Together, we have decided that the policy of opposing the separation of Scotland from the United Kingdom could no longer be sustained.

"We further determined that the future of the United Kingdom would be better served with someone else at the helm of the ship of state. To that end, I will be departing to Buckingham Palace directly after this press conference to offer my resignation to the King. It will be left to my successor to work out the details of Scotland's independent future relationship with the United Kingdom. I can say that it is the intention of both my party and the opposition to enter into negotiations with representatives of the Scottish government with a view to formalising Scotland's future independence, and to work out the details thereof.

"Before coming here today, I ordered the release of anyone who has been detained under the Terrorism Act, who is not directly implicated in a violent crime. This includes all the members of the Scottish Parliament, as well as the mother of Finlay McColl and his friend, Oona MacLean.

"I have also relieved Interim Governor Edward Trentworth of his duties. Authority will rest with the Minister of Defence until such time as a new Interim Governor can be appointed.

"However, there is one important condition to which all parties present at today's meeting agreed. In the interests of the rule of law and public order, negotiations will not commence, nor will Martial Law be suspended, until such time as Staff Sergeant Finlay McColl has surrendered. I call on Sergeant McColl to turn himself in and I guarantee his safe passage and lawful treatment.

"Thank you, I will not be taking questions."

With that, Prime Minister William Gordon turned and walked away, heading towards the side entrance and the waiting Jaguar to take him back to Buckingham Palace, and political oblivion.

BBC News

"This morning, Gregor McAdam, after his release from house arrest last night, appealed publicly to Finlay McColl to turn himself in, repeating former Prime Minister William Gordon's guarantee of safe and fair treatment."

Gregor's face, gaunt and tired, appeared on the screen above rolling headlines, all of them to do with the dramatic developments of the previous 24 hours.

"Finlay McColl is a true Scottish hero. His bravery, coupled with his morality, are the reasons why we are where we are today, on the cusp of freedom. But now, he must pay the price of our freedom with his. I'm appealing to you Finlay, you can come in now son, it's over."

Scottish Highlands, present day

Fin watched with curiosity as the stakeouts set on the Poacher's Pint and his mum's cottage drove away.

He'd been concealed high on the side of the glen for about a week, watching proceedings through a high-power spotting scope. Laying up in an observation post for days on end posed no challenge at all to a trained sniper. He'd subsisted on supplies Stevie snuck up to him when he was out deerstalking, along with the occasional hare or grouse he'd popped with Stevie's .22 rifle.

Even with the obvious watchers leaving, he hoped because it was all over, he still waited till late into the night before heading down into the glen.

No music greeted him when he approached the back of the pub. He took up position near the back door and began to wait, his sniper's patience again coming in handy. Oona would have to come out eventually, to empty a bin or gather some coal for the fire. The screen door at the back eventually creaked open and Oona appeared with two large bin liners full of rubbish.

He stepped forward. "Excuse me miss, would your father like to buy some venison?"

"Fin, you bastard!" she growled, then rushed into waiting arms. He wrapped his arms as far around her as he could get them, ignoring the pain in his shoulder and began to sob like a child.

Fin watched the news with Oona, at Stevie's cottage. It hadn't really been that hard to get there once he'd sailed into Aberdeen. The security forces had all but stood down except in Edinburgh, although they were still lurking around his mother's place. He'd simply 'borrowed' a car and driven there in the dark.

"What are you going to do Fin?"

Fin no longer had the purpose that had stifled all thought and doubt. Now he had to face the music. But his mind worked quickly. He thought he had a way to tidy up one loose end before he ended up in Colchester Prison.

"I can't run Oona, I have to turn myself in."

She didn't cry, she just shook her head. "No, run, I want you to run. Take me with you."

"What about your dad? The pub? Your nursing? And they're looking for any excuse to delay or water down Scottish independence and I can't give it to them. No, I can't do that Oona, I won't run. I'll go. Gregor McAdam will work to get me out. I trust him. I haven't killed anyone." Then he remembered Jimmy, but kept his mouth shut about that. "I'll be out before you know it. Then it's you and me and the pub, together."

She did start crying then and thrust herself into his arms and held onto him tightly, soaking his shirt with her tears.

"I love you Oona. Since I was a boy, I've always loved you."

Edinburgh, Scotland, present day

Gregor sat by the phone, waiting. He had made his appeal, he knew Fin had his number. The deadline for a response was only hours away, 5pm.

The phone rang. God, let it be him.

"Gregor McAdam."

"First Minister, it's Staff Sergeant Finlay McColl."

"Thank God Finlay."

"Yes sir, your orders are for me to come in?"

McAdam paused for a moment. "I won't give you that order son. I won't betray you. I won't be your Sir John, because that would mean just another martyr and this will continue." Fin knew exactly what McAdam meant. Every child in Scotland knew the story of how Sir John of Menteith had sold out William Wallace to the English.

"If I betray you Fin, I believe the killing will continue. But I have to ask you, please come in, for the people of Scotland and nothing less. You are the price of Scotland's freedom. I haven't betrayed you son, I haven't promised them anything or signed you away, I just promised to ask."

Silence.

Finally, "That's sound of you Mr. McAdam, very sound."

Gregor thought he could hear the feint hint of a crack in the man's voice, but couldn't be sure. "It's all I could do. Please son, I have a guarantee of your personal safety and a fair trial for any charges."

"Yes, about that. All it would take is one idiot and I'm dead. I need this to be public, with cameras, the press, everything. Only that would guarantee my safety."

That might work, Gregor thought, that just might do it. He looked at the two men in dark suits sitting across from him, one from the security services and one from No. 10. The politico shrugged, the security man nodded.

"I think that could work Fin, when and where?"

"Tomorrow, 07:00, Castle Esplanade, I'll tell the press if they won't. I'll make sure the cameras are there."

"Okay Fin, I will see what I can do."

"Thank you sir, and two things. One, I will only surrender to my CO, Lachie Sutherland, with Trentworth there."

"I don't know Fin, they would see that as a risk. You might try to kill Trentworth in revenge." He glanced at the security man again who tilted his head and gave a half shake.

Fin spoke first, "I gotta go, call back later." Click.

Fin exited the phone booth and began to play his role.

Gregor turned to security man again, "Were you tracing that?" The guy shrugged. "You fuckers, we need his trust or he won't come in!" and he slammed his hand down.

"Maybe we won't need him to."

"Do you know what this means? You have ruined everything, you fucking twats!"

Duns, Scottish Borders, present day

Miles away in the small Scottish Border town of Duns, a solidly built butch dark haired woman calmly walked away from a phone booth. A pensioner sitting on a bench noted her passing, not attractive, not unattractive, but she knew how to walk for effect. He wouldn't crawl over her to get to his ex-wife, that was for damn sure. No one else gave her a second look as she disappeared around a corner.

Five minutes later an unmarked car cruised by the phone booth, two suits up front. They took a good look at the phone booth where Fin McColl had called McAdam, but saw nothing. They began to search, looping around the side streets.

They found nothing out of the ordinary.

Fin McColl had disappeared.

Edinburgh, Scotland, present day

Gregor's phone rang ten minutes later.

"Tell your mates they're arseholes and if they fuck with me again I swear to God the next bomb I set off will be real. This isn't a fucking game we're playing here. Tell the cunts if I wanted Trentworth dead, he'd already be a rotting corpse. So

would his wife, his daughter and his ugly fucking dog.
Tomorrow. If he's there, it will all be over. If he's not I won't be
shooting up planes next time. Do they think I couldn't get to the
military governor? How about the fucking Prime Minister? Do
they really think I couldn't get to him? I could. I could even get
them, in their safe London homes. But I'll come in Mr. McAdam,
for you and for Scotland. I will pay the price … if Trentworth and
Lachie are there."

The phone clicked again.

Gregor had an irrational and pointless thought that that was
probably the most that Fin McColl had ever said at one time in
his life.

Andy Skeen

Paying the price

The Royal Mile, Edinburgh, Scotland, present day

Helicopters buzzed Edinburgh High Street leading up to Edinburgh Castle. It was called 'The Royal Mile,' because it was about a mile long and ran from Holyrood House, the Royal palace of Scotland, to the ancient military fortification of Edinburgh Palace that dominated the Edinburgh skyline.

Cobbles run most of its length and numerous small medieval alleyways and steps formed a three-dimensional maze of stone on both sides leading up to the Castle Esplanade.

Police, snipers and armoured cars lurked on every rooftop and intersection, while Lachie and Trentworth stood shivering together in overcoats in the centre of the Esplanade.

Fin seemed to appear out of nowhere, walking up the middle of the High Street towards them. He had a pistol carefully taped into his hand with the barrel seemingly taped snugly against the bottom of his jaw. He could easily pull the trigger if they tried to take him before he reached his goal.

The police shadowed him as he walked, but a command decision was made to let him walk. He wore only a t-shirt, despite the cold. They could easily tell that he was not otherwise armed or carrying a bomb. They had him covered with sharpshooters from every angle, if he tried anything, they'd put him down.

Fin smiled as he drew up to the pair, "Sorry to drag you into this Lachie, I just don't trust this fucker."

"I was already in it boy. I'm a Scot too, and absent without leave. Now what the fuck are you playing at? Put the gun down and let's go home. This bastard's been relieved of his duties you know, they found out he had Birt killed."

"I only wanted to look at him one last time. In the eyes."

He turned to Trentworth finally and jumped forward, ripping the gun from jaw and jamming it hard against Trentworth's temple. As he did so, he turned his back to Lachie, so that Lachie became, in effect, a human shield.

"You killed my father you fuck. You and all those other boys. Now you've killed Birt. What does your wife think of you? What about your mother? How can you even stand to look at yourself in the mirror?"

The general snarled, "How dare you, you ignorant little shit, how dare you!"

Fin ground the barrel into Trentworth's head, "You killed my father! I had you in my scope at the Parliament. You could be worm food right now. Why shouldn't I finish the job now, for Birt. For my father?"

Trentworth's gaze snapped up, "Son—"

"I'm not your son!"

All around the esplanade fingers tightened on the triggers of numerous guns aimed right at Fin's head.

He'd been deceiving himself. From the moment he'd left Oona's dad's pub the day they'd announced Trentworth was being put in charge of Scotland, he thought he was in control, calling the shots. He hadn't felt a thing, hadn't thought about it, he'd just acted. Now he felt that control slipping away.

He'd killed many times, men and deer, but he'd never enjoyed the kill. Always the stalk, but never the kill. Now, he knew he was about to kill for pleasure. He wanted this man's brains splattered on the ground, to smell the tang of his blood in the air and the stink as his bowels relaxed after a lifetime of clinching.

Lachie noticed. He saw how tightly Fin gripped the pistol, how hard he clinched his jaw. He knew this was going to end badly and started to plan what he might have to do, when Trentworth spoke.

"Sergeant McColl, I've got nothing left. If you're going to kill me, do it. You've won, they sacked me, my career is over. Whether you believe this or not, I know I'm responsible for what happened to those men out on Tumbledown, I was there remember? Sergeant Singhe was an accident, I am sorry. Scotland is going to have its beloved independence and I'm finished. So hurry up and do what ever it is you're going to do."

Fin stared at Trentworth and thought about his dad, Birt, Oona, and Jimmy. He gripped the pistol tighter and took up the slack in the trigger, right to the point of the sear breaking. He knew he didn't have much time before a sniper got the green light to take him with a headshot.

Policemen edged closer, automatic weapons tucked tightly to their shoulders, all tight on Fin's head. Powerful cameras zoomed in on the faces of all three men.

"You get to live Trentworth. You get to see those boys' faces every night when you lay down to sleep. You get to live because of your son and because of your wife. You get to struggle to remember what your boy's face looks like every day, like I struggle to remember my father's face. And you will some day rot in hell."

He lowered the pistol and turned slowly to the nearest policeman, "It's not loaded."

They rushed forward, obeying a silent command in their earpieces, taking him to the ground. Reporters pushed forward from where they had crouched behind cars and police vans, breaking through police lines to get close to their quarry, yelling questions.

As they dragged and pushed Fin away, he managed to turn and face them.

He had a mischievous look on his face as the photographers snapped away.

He threw his head back, shouting at the sky in his best imitation of Mel Gibson doing an imitation of a Scot, "FREEDOM!!"

Whore no more

House of commons, London, England, present day

The House of Commons resembled nothing less than a colony of penguins huddled together against the Antarctic winter, packed shoulder to shoulder to share their warmth.

"Madam Speaker," the Clerk began, "On the motion to dissolve the Union of Parliaments Act of 1707, ayes 378, nays 249—".

The House burst into chaos, some cheering, many angry, but most just looking grim. Several ministers on both sides of the aisle threw their Order Papers in the air or into the aisle, adding to the general chaos.

"—The aye's have it!" the Speaker shouted over the roar.

In cities and towns around Scotland, in pubs, in their living rooms, and in town centres, dour hardened men broke down and cried like little children and hugged strangers like long-lost friends. In Edinburgh around the Parliament Building, crowds broke into song, The Flower of Scotland, shouting more than singing. Bagpipes played Scotland the Brave from hilltops and on street corners.

Fin's mum and Oona watched the telly in the Poacher's Pint with the cheering crowd, they hugged, crying. Fin watched in prison with loads of other Scots arrested during the uprising and their cheers deafened the guards.

They'd done it, it was real.

The next day's Scotsman carried a half page photograph of Fin shouting, under a half page banner headline: FREEDOM!

Over the next weeks and months the papers ran a series of historic headlines:

McColl to face Court Martial

Trentworth charged with negligent homicide

Scotland recognised by UN, EU

Singhe killers may never be known

Epilogue—some years later ...

Outside the Scottish Parliament, Edinburgh, Scotland

A fifteen-foot bronze statue of Fin and Birt now stands proudly in front of the Scottish Parliament.

Staring curiously up at the statue, 8-year old Lorna MacDonald asks her mother, "Who's that Mummy?"

"That's Fin McColl and Sabjirt Singhe. Before you were born, they helped Scotland gain its freedom."

With a child's simple directness she asks, "Are they dead now?"

"Well, Birt has gone to heaven, but no one knows what happened to Finlay. He was in prison for a while down in England, but he escaped years ago.

The Australian Outback

The quad bike roars through the Australian bush dodging trees. It screeches to a halt. Finlay is at the wheel, with Oona clinging tightly to his back. She has a rifle on her shoulder.

A grunting squealing mass of black fury erupts from the bush ahead, a massive wild boar heading straight at them, cornered and angry.

Finlay shouts, "SHOOT!"

Oona takes careful aim at the charging boar and eases back the trigger just like she'd been taught, completely free of panic.

The End

About the author

Andy Skeen immigrated to the UK in 1998 to marry. He and his wife lived in Edinburgh for many years, but now live outside London, where he works as a professional copywriter. He previously studied or worked in Japan, Hawaii, Italy, Idaho and Washington State. He holds a BA in Asian Studies/Economics, and an MA and most of a PhD in Asian History.

When not slaving away at a desk, he spends his time target shooting, tinkering in his workshop or reading military, political and social history. He won the 'Any Rifle Sniper' category at the 2007 Scottish National Historical Rifle Championship held at the Ministry of Defence range in the Pentland Hills, south of Edinburgh.

5825187R00158

Printed in Great Britain
by Amazon.co.uk, Ltd.,
Marston Gate.